"I trust you."

She'd meant the words to be innocent, but as he reached out to take the container from her, his hands overlapped hers. Whether by accident or design, she didn't know. She didn't care.

Time stopped.

The comfort Maggie had felt in Billy Corrigan's presence during the past four days was replaced by something different, something more. Attraction wrapped around her like a cloud of incense—seductive, heady, dangerous. She raised her head and met his eyes, which had turned from ice-gray to the color of a mountain lake. Then her gaze went to his mouth.

He took his hands away. She blinked and stepped back as the moment was broken.

She couldn't possibly afford to get involved with him when everyone around her seemed to wind up dead.

Dear Harlequin Intrigue Reader,

At Harlequin Intrigue we have much to look forward to as we ring in a brand-new year. Case in point—all of our romantic suspense selections this month are fraught with edge-of-your-seat danger, electrifying romance and thrilling excitement. So hang on!

Reader favorite Debra Webb spins the next installment in her popular series COLBY AGENCY. *Cries in the Night* spotlights a mother so desperate to track down her missing child that she joins forces with the unforgettable man from her past.

Unsanctioned Memories by Julie Miller—the next offering in THE TAYLOR CLAN—packs a powerful punch as a vengeance-seeking FBI agent opens his heart to the achingly vulnerable lone witness who can lead him to a cold-blooded killer.... Looking for a provocative mystery with a royal twist? Then expect to be seduced by Jacqueline Diamond in *Sheikh Surrender*.

We welcome two talented debut authors to Harlequin Intrigue this month. Tracy Montoya weaves a chilling mystery in *Maximum Security*, and the gripping *Concealed Weapon* by Susan Peterson is part of our BACHELORS AT LARGE promotion.

Finally this month, Kasi Blake returns to Harlequin Intrigue with *Borrowed Identity*. This gothic mystery will keep you guessing when a groggy bride stumbles upon a grisly murder on her wedding night. But are her eyes deceiving her when her "slain" groom appears alive and well in a flash of lightning?

It promises to be quite a year at Harlequin Intrigue....

Enjoy!

Denise O'Sullivan
Senior Editor
Harlequin Intrigue

MAXIMUM
SECURITY
TRACY MONTOYA

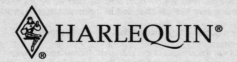

TORONTO • NEW YORK • LONDON
AMSTERDAM • PARIS • SYDNEY • HAMBURG
STOCKHOLM • ATHENS • TOKYO • MILAN • MADRID
PRAGUE • WARSAW • BUDAPEST • AUCKLAND

ISBN 0-373-22750-7

MAXIMUM SECURITY

Copyright © 2004 by Tracy Fernandez Rysavy

This edition published by arrangement with Harlequin Books S.A.

® and TM are trademarks of the publisher. Trademarks indicated with ® are registered in the United States Patent and Trademark Office, the Canadian Trade Marks Office and in other countries.

Visit us at www.eHarlequin.com

Printed in U.S.A.

ABOUT THE AUTHOR

Debut Intrigue author Tracy Montoya is a magazine editor for a nonprofit outfit in Washington, D.C., though at present she's telecommuting from her house in Seoul, Korea. She lives with a psychotic cat, a lovable yet daft Lhasa apso and a husband who's turned their home into the Island of Lost/Broken/Strange-Looking Antiques. A member of the National Association of Hispanic Journalists and the Society of Environmental Journalists, Tracy has written about everything from Booker Prize–winning poet Martín Espada to socially responsible mutual funds to soap opera summits. Her articles have appeared in a variety of publications, such as *Hope, Utne Reader, Satya, YES!, Natural Home* and *New York Naturally*. Prior to launching her journalism career, she taught in an underresourced school in Louisiana through the AmeriCorps Teach for America program.

Tracy holds a master's degree in English literature from Boston College and a B.A. in the same from St. Mary's University. When she's not writing, she likes to scuba dive, forget to go to kickboxing class, wallow in bed with a good book, or get out her new guitar with a group of friends and pretend she's Suzanne Vega.

She loves to hear from readers—e-mail TracyMontoya@aol.com or visit www.tracymontoya.com.

Books by Tracy Montoya

HARLEQUIN INTRIGUE
750—MAXIMUM SECURITY

CAST OF CHARACTERS

Maggie Reyes—A bestselling true-crime writer, Maggie has served on criminal task forces because of her first-rate research and sharp memory for details. Now one of her past subjects—an infamous serial killer—has made her the object of his brutal fixation.

Billy Corrigan—The loner FBI agent is going outside his investigative territory to bring down the man who murdered his sister. His search for vengeance leads him to the one woman who survived the vicious killer's obsession.

The Surgeon—Always one step ahead of the authorities, this psychopath has stalked and murdered women across four states. Now he's set his focus entirely on one woman—and the only thing standing between him and Maggie Reyes is a rogue FBI agent with a taste for revenge.

Adriana Torres—A friend from Maggie's college days, Adriana has done everything she can for the past eighteen months to keep Maggie hidden from the Surgeon—but will her selflessness put her life in jeopardy?

James Brentwood—Adriana's lover, local police detective James Brentwood is willing to put his own life on the line to stop the man who murdered nine women from killing again.

Elizabeth Borkowski—James Brentwood's wisecracking partner, she knows Billy from way back. The no-nonsense detective wants to help Maggie, but she wonders whether or not to believe the woman's unlikely tale of a serial killer who stalks across state lines.

To Tom and Ana Rysavy.
Thank you for that rarest of gifts—
a truly wonderful childhood.
(Well, except for that whole sharing one bottle of soda
thing, but we'll just not mention it.)

Chapter One

He was coming for her.

The now-familiar ache of dread crept through her body as Maggie Reyes traced her finger around the photo of the smilng girl's face—a photo that now graced the front page of the *Monterey County Herald* with the words *victim* and *homicide* buried in the caption. Four murders in four states in four months. And now he was only minutes away.

Why don't you run?

Maggie placed her palms flat on her desk and pushed herself up to a standing position. It was funny, even though her head was telling her to run and the fear in her heart robbed her of sleep every night, that odd sense of security she always felt in her cousin Esme's Monterey beach home was still there. Raising her eyes to the map of the United States above her, Maggie fished a red-tipped thumbtack out of the wooden caddy meticulously placed in the upper left corner of the desk. Little Rock. St. Louis. Denver. All three cities had red tacks plunged through the center of their black dots on the map. And they had fat, corresponding files in the metal cabinet to her left, filled with articles from the dozens of newspapers she subscribed to, printouts from database searches, posts from a few true-crime listservs and other odds and ends pertaining to the cases. In one swift motion, Maggie pushed the fourth tack through Carmel-by-the-Sea, California, releasing the breath she'd been holding as she did so.

Carmel, sister city to Monterey, which she now called home.

Do you wanna live forever, Maggie?

Ignoring the persistent whisper inside her head, she turned her back on the map and padded across the plush Berber rug to the window seat in what she had come to think of as ''her'' office, where she could watch the white-capped waves break against the jagged black rocks jutting up toward the sky like sentinels. Monterey, California, was a beautiful, sunny city, except for in a few areas along the water that had their own peculiar micro-climates. The house Maggie lived in lay smack in the middle of one of them and was always enveloped in fog and mist. Not that it really mattered.

Folding herself into the small nook, she leaned against a wooden support and dug her bare toes into the brocade seat cushion. Her gaze wandered farther down the beach, past the point where the black rocks and dark, foamy water abruptly ended and a few intrepid surfers were paddling toward the horizon in search of the next big wave. Thinking of the wet suit that hadn't seen action since the late '90s, she listened to the muffled roar of the ocean and watched the surfers for what felt like fifteen minutes. When at last she glanced at the glowing red numbers of the digital clock on her desk, she found it was three-thirty. It had been over two hours.

How time flies when you're stuck at home with no place to go.

Or when you're avoiding something. Maggie's fingers toyed with the slight fringe around the hole in the knee of her jeans. Gee, fringe. That could keep her busy for half a day if she let it.

And that was the thing. She couldn't let it anymore. Four killings in four months, and every single one of them weighing on her conscience like stone. And now he was coming for her.

And now there was no one to call, nowhere to run. Esme was safe in her other home in Seattle, and Maggie had left her family in New Orleans, safe in their complete ignorance of her whereabouts. She routed letters through Esme to her parents or risked the occasional phone call through her alias Mary Smythe's long-distance account, but that was all the communication she'd risk. Not the ideal arrangement, but there was no way she wanted anyone close to her in danger.

But now the impulse to bolt out the door and run for home as far and as fast as she could was almost overpowering. Almost. But once upon a time, she'd been a cop, not the silly caretaker of her rich cousin's beach house. And she would have laughed if anyone had told her she'd be hiding thousands of miles away from her Louisiana home—in California, of all places—with blond hair and an assumed name. Mary Smythe-with-a-Y. She snorted as she rose from the window seat. At least she could have had the wherewithal to choose something more glamorous. She walked into the hallway and caught a glimpse of herself in the antique mirror hanging near the front door. Thank God she'd asked Adriana for a box of Revlon Rich Auburn-Black 22 when she'd made out this week's grocery list. The color suited her skin tone; she was never meant to be a blond.

Taking a deep breath, Maggie turned her head, gripped the brass handle of the ornate wooden door. With one push of her finger, one swing of her arm, she could be outside, just a mile away from sunshine and people walking their dogs, hand-dipped ice cream and a real bookstore. Only three miles away from the Monterey police station, ten from the gruesome murder she'd just read about in the papers.

Her hand started to shake, just a slight tremor, and she closed her eyes. One push, one swing. She had a job to do, and after a year and a half of insanity, she was going to do it. If anyone was going to stop the Surgeon's murdering spree, they were going to need her. It was time for Miss Mary Smythe to stop being the crazy woman on the beach, time for her to rejoin the living, time for her to be fearless Maggie Reyes again.

Maggie pushed, Maggie swung.

And a hurricane-grade wind lashed through the hall. It whipped around the mirror, toppled the coat tree, sent the car keys that hung unused on a small nail crashing to the floor.

"Oh, God!" Maggie gasped, and then she couldn't breathe, couldn't think. Something was wrapping itself around her neck, strangling her, and she clawed at her throat with frantic hands, trying to loosen whatever it was so she could breathe again. Tighter and tighter and tighter, until all she could see was black.

Her knees crashed to the hardwood floor, and she groped blindly outward until she felt the doorjamb beneath her fingers. Her other hand swung out and connected with the open door. The pressure on her windpipe eased a little, just enough for her to take one last gasp and use the tiny trickle of energy it gave her to heave the door closed.

She could still hear her own heartbeat, thundering in her ears while she took deep, gasping gulps of air. The invisible hands gently caressed her throat as they uncoiled, reminding her that they were still there. Waiting. And then they were gone.

Shaking, she turned her body around until she was sitting on the floor, her back leaning against the door, barring it from ever opening again and sending her tattered remains of sanity whirling out with the afternoon breeze. She rested her hands on her knees, watching as the tremors slowed, and then stopped. Listened to her heart return to its normal pattern, her breathing slow to a smooth, almost meditative rhythm. Her eyes darted to the coat tree standing straight and tall in the hallway corner; her keys hung on their nail by the mirror, undisturbed. Welcome to the grand delusion.

A single chime from the grandfather clock that shared the hallway with her was all it took to completely bring her back to the land of the living.

Four-thirty. She had a half hour before the police detective Adriana had recommended went home for the day.

Better try the phone, Miss Mary

MAGGIE WAS STILL sitting on the floor, cordless phone in hand, when the knock came. Darn. She knew she'd stayed on the phone too long leaving her ''anonymous tip'' with the Monterey police. Of course they'd traced it to her alias Mary Smythe's account and were coming to ask her questions. The last thing she wanted was to be dealing with their questions—the same kind that had sent her spiraling down into her mad, mad world in the first place. Maybe if she just sat there and made herself as small and still as she could, the cops would go away.

Another knock came, harder and more insistent this time. Maggie gently put the phone on the ground and hugged her knees to her chest. *Just go away. Just leave me alone.*

No such luck. The next knock rattled her bones through the solid wood of the door. ''Oh, go have a doughnut,'' she mumbled, though she flexed her legs and slid her spine upward along the wall until she was standing. Resigning herself to the fact that she would have to face the police sooner or later, she turned to look through the peephole.

Odd. Rather than the casual business attire most of Monterey's finest preferred, the man on her doorstep wore faded jeans and a dusty-blue T-shirt with the words *Got Mojo?* scrawled across his broad back in white letters.

"Charming," she muttered, then cupped her hands around her mouth. "Got ID?" she shouted through the door.

He turned, shoulders arched back with the easy grace of an athlete, and Maggie sucked in a breath. Okay, so maybe the man had a little mojo. His still, gray eyes narrowed, and a corner of his mouth turned upward in an amused smirk, further accentuated by the pronounced bow-shaped curve to his upper lip. Okay, so he was cute. Being a white male between the ages of 30 and 35, the guy was also solidly in the demographic that included most of your average serial killers.

Which was not something Maggie took lightly anymore.

She watched him reach behind him to grab something out of his back pocket—and jumped back in surprise when his wallet smacked against the peephole, obliterating the tiny spot of light that usually shone through the door.

He drew the wallet back, and she moved closer once again, giving his badge—all she could see given her limited range of vision—as thorough a once-over as she could.

"I'm looking for Mary Smythe." His voice was low and soft, even through the door, but with the faintest rough edge to it. Politely dangerous. It didn't sound familiar, but then, there was a lot about her past that she'd worked hard to block out of memory.

Maggie leaned her forehead against the door, weighing her options. Would the Surgeon knock on her door in broad daylight? Improbable, given his preference for nighttime ambushes and drugs that stole your ability to reason.

The thought nearly caused Maggie to slide to the floor once more, but then she realized that there was no way the man on her doorstep could compare to the monsters inside her head, anyway. She'd never been afraid to face a threat head-on—it was living in constant fear of being watched, taken by surprise, attacked from behind that made her crazy. With a defiant snap of her wrist, she shot back the deadbolt and opened the door, careful to keep it between her body and the outside world. As soon as he'd stepped into the entryway, she pushed it shut again. And exhaled.

He didn't say a word once they were face-to-face, almost scowling as he gave her a thorough scrutinizing with those pale gray eyes of his. Apparently, she'd surprised him by not being seventy-something, with rollers in her hair and twenty cats sweeping around her ankles. But he quickly got his face under control, shoving a hand through his thick brown hair so it spiked slightly.

"So. You must be James Brentwood, then," she said a little too loudly, folding her arms and widening her eyes in an attempt to look as unhinged as possible. One good thing about being the crazy woman on Mermaid Point—no one expected you to waste time with social graces. And they usually were only too happy to leave you alone as soon as possible.

"That's right." He quickly flashed his badge once more, then folded up the wallet and jammed it into his back pocket. "Ma'am. I'm sorry to bother you, but I'm here about an anonymous phone call placed from this location at 4:37 p.m."

A short silence stretched between them as they each pondered their next moves, like two grand masters over a chessboard. Maggie circled around him and took her time picking the cordless phone off the floor, placing it back in its cradle while her eyes darted ever so briefly to the panic button on her security system's white keypad. "I thought the point of leaving an anonymous tip was that one remained anonymous," she finally said.

"Usually," he said. "But not with something like this, ma'am."

"I'm not much older than you, so if you don't stop ma'am-ing me, I might be forced to start screaming like a lunatic, right here, right now." To her satisfaction, he blinked, apparently wondering whether or not she was serious. Good. Best to keep him on edge so she had the advantage. She so needed to remain in control of this conversation.

It didn't take him long to recover. "I'll call you Sheena, Queen of the Jungle, if it helps you answer my questions," he said.

"Spare me your fantasies. Mary will do." Well. Obviously she hadn't made him *that* uncomfortable. "So you're Brentwood, the one I talked to on the phone?"

At his nod, she motioned him ahead of her, into the spacious kitchen just beyond the entryway. "Come in. I was going to make coffee."

"Nice place." The man's eyes skimmed over the room's pale wood cabinets, ceramic tiles, and state-of-the-art steel appliances. A little too minimalist Pottery Barn for her taste, but she couldn't be picky when Esme was willing to put a roof with an ocean view over her unproductive head.

The rest of Brentwood's body remained almost preternaturally still. And despite the badge, the cop's attention to detail, the standard issue semi-automatic Glock prominently displayed in the shoulder holster, Maggie felt the hair on the back of her neck prickle.

Maybe it was just the small gold hoop in his left ear, maybe it was the too-casual clothes, the too-relaxed stance, but she couldn't shake the feeling that something was really, really wrong here.

He's a cop, Reyes. Get a grip, she chided herself. However, the thought wasn't enough to keep her from casually sidling to the left so the large kitchen island was between them. She gestured for him to sit down...in the chair farthest from her.

"Well, Mary, you mind if we get started?" he asked. The hoarse quality to his voice made the mundane phrase sound almost X-rated. And that was a little too much for a healthy woman in her early 30s who had been celibate for…way too long.

Even so, her overactive hormones weren't quite enough to make her overlook the absence of an evidence-gathering notebook in his hands.

"So. Coffee, Officer Brentwood?" she asked, taking the glass pot out of the coffeemaker to her right and filling it up with water. "Adriana brought some Kona beans from her last trip to Hawaii. I haven't tried it yet, but she says it's wonderful."

"Adriana's your neighbor?" he asked.

Maggie glanced out the windows, past the patio she never used, and watched the waves break against the rocks for a moment. "A friend," she murmured, biting her lower lip. The rush of cool water over the hand holding the pot brought her attention back to her task.

"Mary, I don't want to be rude…"

Here it comes.

"…but you said on the phone you believe a serial killer called the Surgeon might have left his New Orleans territory and is on his way to Monterey. Since that's all you felt like telling us, I'm here to find out what gave you that impression."

Reaching for the blue ceramic sugar canister, Maggie undid the metal clasp and peeled the sealed lid back, stuffing her hand inside. Out of the corner of her eye, she saw that the man had stood and was leaning against the table, facing her. "I'm sorry, officer. I don't mean to waste your time—"

With that, Maggie pulled her hand out of the canister and swung around. She switched off the safety of her Firestar M43 and aimed the small gun right for his mojo-covered heart. "But if you're James Brentwood, then I really am Sheena, Queen of the Jungle."

Chapter Two

"So we're even." With that disturbingly cryptic statement, the man's voice seemed to go a couple of octaves deeper than it had been, sending goosebumps down her arms for all the wrong reasons. He slowly raised his hands, keeping his elbows close in by his sides.

"I'm not even going to dignify that with a response, Stalker Boy." She kept the Firestar aimed at his chest, adrenaline making her peripheral vision narrow until all she could see was him over the sights of her gun. "Just put your weapon on the floor and keep your hands where I can see them, because I will not hesitate to shoot you if you even *breathe* too hard in my direction."

"How did you—?"

"Drop. The. Gun." She gestured impatiently with her own weapon. "Now."

He complied, stretching his arm out to drop his Glock as close to her as possible. "Okay, it's on the floor. I'm not here to hurt you," he said, never taking those still, gray eyes off her.

"Whatever. Now the one on your ankle."

He shook his head. "I don't have—"

"Spare me. Your leg drags when you walk."

With a hiss of breath, he bent over and pushed up the frayed hem of his faded jeans, unstrapping the small .38 from the ankle holster she'd known was there. He casually tossed the gun aside, sending it skittering across the ceramic tiles and through the arched doorway into the formal dining room. Then, raising his palms, he opened his eyes wide with what she was fast beginning to realize was his "trust me" look—which really wasn't working. "I'm not here to hurt you," he repeated.

"Great," Maggie responded calmly, trying not to think about what was going to happen to her nerves once the adrenaline high wore off. "Then why don't you sit down in that chair and tell me who the hell you are?"

"Billy Corrigan, FBI Computer Crimes Division."

"*Get* your hand back up where I can see it," Maggie snapped as Billy's hand froze on its way to his back pocket. "Back up in the air, there we go." Making a wide circle around the table, she stopped directly behind the chair nearest the small mission-style phone table. All telephones in the house were programmed to dial 911 at the push of a button, and it couldn't hurt her to be as near one of them as possible. "I don't want to see your ID, Billy Corrigan, if that's really your name."

"It is," he replied calmly. "But it's funny. You don't look like a Mary Smythe."

"Says you." Her gun arm was beginning to grow tired, probably from the months—no, years now—she'd been off active duty. She tightened her grip on the Firestar, hoping he wouldn't notice that her hands were shaking.

He shrugged, the casual gesture belying the intensity of his pale eyes as they skimmed across her face, seemingly memorizing it. "Black hair, nice tan, despite living under constant cloud cover. You look more like a Maria."

"So my parents are Honduran. So what?"

"In fact, I'd even say you look exactly like a Magdalena. Don't you think, Maggie Reyes?" he asked softly, pinning her with those other-worldly eyes just as surely as if he'd slammed a hand against her throat.

Maggie gasped, backing into the kitchen counter so suddenly, she felt a burst of pain as the edge jabbed into the small of her back. "How—?"

"I read all your books," he said, anticipating her question. "Including the author bio. You were a cop for four years before you turned to crime writing full-time. You've written eight true crime books for a major publisher, about half of which have landed on some bestseller list somewhere. You used to have a dog named Andromeda, although I don't see any evidence of her here. And you like surfing and any other sport connected with water."

Maggie could only stare at him, unsure whether to be impressed or deeply frightened.

"I recognized you from the book jacket photo,"

Corrigan continued. He hitched one shoulder in a singular shrug. "Nice shot. It does you justice."

Before she could react, he reached into his back pocket and pulled out his wallet, tossing it on the table so it landed with a loud smack. It fell open, the large, blue FBI at the top of the ID she'd never gotten a solid glimpse of reassuring her slightly.

"You'll find a business card inside with Fay Parker's name on it," he said. "She's the SAC of the San Francisco field office. Call her. She'll tell you I'm legit." Corrigan sat down and leaned back in one of her kitchen chairs, lazily stretching his lean, denim-encased legs out in front of him.

SAC. It took her a few minutes to remember that the acronym meant Special Agent in Charge. Darn, it had been a while since she'd been in the game. Maggie tore her gaze away from the man's wallet on the table, keeping the gun between them as she tried hard to keep her fear under control. "I don't understand what you're doing here. If you're assigned to the San Francisco office, why would a serial killer who, until now, has stuck to his Louisiana territory, interest you?" She braced her tiring right elbow on the Formica and shot him what she hoped was a skeptical look. "Especially if you're in Computer Crimes. What're you going to do if you find him—throw old motherboards at him?"

Before she could react, he sprang out of the chair and pinned her with his body against the counter. She instinctively raised her hands to protect her face, a whimper escaping her lips before she could quell it.

She didn't even notice that the Firestar was no longer in her possession until she heard the magazine clatter to the floor, soon followed by a sharp clink indicating he'd ejected the chambered round as well.

"I'll figure something out," he said softly, making her all too conscious of just how vulnerable she was.

"Get out," Maggie whispered, disgusted with herself. That wouldn't have happened to her two years ago, when she'd been in the best shape of her life—and most likely able to defend herself against the charms of a too-handsome man with scary reflexes. She swiped her hand at the empty gun he held over their heads, knowing as she did so that it was a futile gesture.

It was. Instead, Maggie contented herself with wrapping her hands under his left wrist, which was braced against the counter. With a speed that came from years of training and eighteen months with nothing better to do, she brought the arch of her foot down hard along his shin, ending the move by crunching her weight down on his instep. In the split second where Corrigan slightly lost his balance, Maggie pushed back on his wrist, ducking under his arm and finally pinning it to his back at an awkward angle.

"You like to play rough, Maggie?" he asked through gritted teeth.

Jerk. She pushed the offending limb into an even more impossible position. "Drop my gun. Drop it now, or I'll break your arm," she snarled.

He dropped the Firestar, but twisted out of her

grasp when her attention was momentarily drawn to the fallen weapon.

"Okay," he said, backing away from her and holding his hands out so his palms faced her. "Okay. There's no reason to get upset. I need your help, Maggie. I swear, that's the honest truth. I never meant to frighten you."

"Right," she retorted. "So your whole 'speak softly and flash a big gun' schtick was meant to be reassuring? Was this before or after you were going to stop impersonating an officer and tell me who you really were?"

"Maggie—"

"Stop using my name so much. You sound like a used car salesman." She advanced toward him and nearly stepped on the Glock she'd made him discard when he first came into the kitchen. She kicked it savagely across the room, far out of reach of either of them. A strand of black hair fell across her forehead and she blew it back in a huff. "You're not going to be in my house long enough to establish any sort of rapport with me, so get used to it."

He stopped backing away. "I'm not lying to you now. I am with the FBI. My badge is right there. You can trust me."

"A lot of women trusted Kenneth Bianchi, Paul Bernardo, Ted Bundy. All good-looking, charming men." Finally next to the kitchen phone again, Maggie snatched the receiver out of its cradle. "Homicidal maniacs, the lot of them."

"Maggie—" She cut him off with a sharp glare.

He cleared his throat and tried again. "I believe you. About the Surgeon coming here."

Her finger hovered over the automatic dial button, but his words stopped her cold.

"Elizabeth Borkowski, a detective with the Monterey PD, is married to an old friend of mine from school. She knows about my interest in this case," he continued, his eyes never leaving hers. "Do you really think the police are going to pay attention to you otherwise, without proof? Liz told me they'd filed your tip."

Maggie dropped the receiver back in its cradle, feeling her entire body slump a bit at his words. She wrapped her arms tightly around her body, as if literally holding herself together while the adrenaline drained away as quickly as it had come.

"But I noticed the similarities between the New Orleans murders and the Carmel murder." He closed the gap between them and placed a hand gently on her arm. Comforting, not threatening. A good way to approach the mentally unstable. "And when the cops at the Monterey station mentioned Little Rock, St. Louis and Denver, I plugged in my laptop and pulled up the files," he said. "I knew you were on to something. But I didn't expect..." He paused, cleared his throat. "You."

"You expected Mary Smythe." She looked down at where he had touched her. It was just a gesture, she told herself. Just meant to inspire trust now that there was a tenuous connection between them. "The crazy woman on Mermaid Point."

He searched her face, probably trying to ascertain her craziness for himself. "I'm sorry."

"It doesn't matter." Maggie hitched her shoulder abruptly, shrugging his hand off her, surprised when she missed the warmth of his touch once she was free.

"You're not crazy." His low voice wrapped around her, making her feel almost safe for the first time in two years. "I don't know what made those cops think so, but I know your work. You have one of the best research minds out there. I saw you at Quantico."

Where she'd given several guest lectures. She turned to look out the window at the waves, tugging on the end of her braid. *Oh, God, make him stop.*

"You blew my mind."

Bringing her hand up to her forehead, Maggie pinched the bridge of her nose, trying to harden herself to his words.

As if sensing how close she was to her breaking point, he asked, "Case in point, how'd you know I wasn't James Brentwood? Liz said no one at the station has ever met you."

She took a moment before responding, praying her voice would come out strong and steady, even though she didn't feel that way. "*Detective* James Brentwood is a fidgeter." He flinched at her emphasis on detective, since he'd answered to *officer*. She gave him a small smile of sympathy and continued. "On the phone you can hear him clicking pens or drumming his fingers while he talks. You've barely moved since you came in. And you didn't know who Adriana was. I took a chance.''

She turned and met his gaze. He raised a questioning eyebrow at her.

''James's girlfriend of five months,'' she said. ''She's a friend of mine, which is why I asked specifically for him.''

''Damn.''

''Yeah.'' They stared at each other for a long moment, the silence stretching between them.

''Why do they—?'' He stopped, obviously aware that the question he was about to ask was too familiar, too much of a breach of civility. She finished it for him.

''Think I'm crazy? Try whisking me out of the house for a wild night on the town. You'll find out in about two seconds.''

''Tempting offer.''

She whirled on him, not in the mood to flirt no matter what her sarcastic comment had implied. ''Get out,'' she said with more venom than she'd meant to deliver. Her vision blurred, and she closed her eyes to stop the sudden tears from spilling out of them. She rubbed a hand against her cheekbone. ''I've got something in my contact lens,'' she lied.

''Maggie—''

She flinched when he took a step toward her, his hand outstretched as if to comfort her. Heaven help her, she was so far beyond comforting. ''Get out of my house, Agent Corrigan. You lost any amount of trust I had in you when you brought two weapons into my home and lied to me.''

''I'm sorry,'' he said softly.

She wrapped her arms around herself and dropped her gaze to the floor, all of her tough-girl pretenses gone. She figured they'd been transparent enough anyway. ''Just go.''

Corrigan grabbed his wallet and pulled a card out of it, pressing the small piece of paper onto the bleached wood of the table. ''If anything—'' He paused. ''If anything happens, if you need anything, call me. My cell phone number is at the bottom.''

She snorted in response.

He stepped close, so close, until leaning forward just an inch would have brought their bodies into contact. ''I'll be there,'' he said, and she could feel his breath on her cheek.

''Why is this so important to you?'' she asked, focusing her gaze on his elbow.

The almost gentle air he'd had abruptly vanished as tension simmered through his frame. He spun around and stalked away, pausing only to pick up his weapons before he headed for the door. Despite the fact that she knew she shouldn't, Maggie followed, careful to stand to the side when he wrenched it open. ''Remember the Riverwalk?'' he asked suddenly, his back to her. ''The one he took in broad daylight?''

''Jenna—'' she paused, almost choking over the next word as understanding dawned ''—Corrigan.''

His head turned so she could see a glimpse of his

profile in the blinding ray of light streaming in from the outside. ''My sister.''

And then he vanished behind the door, to a place where she couldn't follow.

Chapter Three

Billy floored the accelerator of his FBI-issue Crown Victoria sedan, zipping down Highway 101 as he headed toward San Francisco. Parker was going to have his ass if he didn't submit that electronic search affadavit for the DigiSystems case. But first, he had one more stop to make. Those computer files weren't going anywhere.

As he approached the city and his exit, he brought the pale tan car to a slow crawl behind the stalled traffic, his thoughts returning once more to Maggie Reyes. Beautiful, crazy Maggie Reyes. The only woman to survive the Surgeon's lethal obsession. But had her brilliant, analytical mind survived?

With everything he'd read about the attack, he couldn't exactly blame her if she wasn't the same afterward. The newspapers had bled all the terror out of her story, leaving only the ugly, sensational words guaranteed to sell papers—phrases like *severe head trauma* and *blitz attack,* coupled with entire paragraphs about how the Surgeon had carried her into the Atchafalaya and sliced off her dark business suit with a sharp knife, leaving shallow cuts marring her once-perfect skin. He'd seen the photos. *Nightmare* didn't even begin to describe it. That she'd managed to escape said a lot about how strong she was.

But then there were the rumors he'd heard—whispers of paralyzing fear and even agoraphobia echoed in the classrooms and auditoriums where she'd conducted her famous lectures. For two years, there had been no more books from Maggie Reyes. No more talks. She'd simply disappeared without a trace.

Until now.

Although he'd been deliberately vague about how he'd found her, to avoid freaking her out any more than he already had, he'd actually been looking for Maggie Reyes for some time.

Billy could find just about anyone, as long as the person used a computer hooked up to the outside world. Most people, he'd learned, simply trusted that no one was watching when they logged on. A few months ago, he'd released some specially modified search bots into the Internet, where they'd floated out in the ether, just waiting for one Maggie Reyes to log on anytime, anyplace, and enter her name and address. A few weeks ago, she'd purchased a copy of *Through the Looking Glass* from an online bookstore, and the bots had come running back to daddy with the news. Child's play.

And now that he'd found her, practically in his backyard all this time, could he get her to trust him? Her assumption that he was Monterey PD had bought him an invitation inside her home and enough time to assess her state of mind, but it probably hadn't been such a great idea if he wanted her to warm up to him. Truth was, he wasn't supposed to be poking his nose in cases that had nothing to do with Computer Crimes, and he needed someone outside the system to help him get the man who'd attacked his sister. He needed Maggie Reyes.

But he hadn't expect her to be so—

The cars ahead of him suddenly lurched forward, and he abruptly shoved aside thoughts of the woman he'd left behind. Jenna was all that mattered. The image of his sister, her pale, crumpled body covered in blood and grime, came to him in mercilessly clear focus, just as it always did whenever he said or thought her name. Jenna. Jenna. Jenna.

How that image had haunted him, haunted him still. He'd gotten distracted by a case in Silicon Valley. He'd been so close to bringing down the CEO of a high-powered software company on computer embezzlement. So he'd postponed a trip to New Orleans to see his sister, the only remaining member of his immediate family. Then he'd gotten the phone call.

Blitz attack.... He turned down Van Buren Street, the words coming back to him with so much more force than they had when they'd merely been black ink on newsprint. *...heavy blood loss...so sorry....* With a sharp twist of his hand, Billy jerked the steering wheel, threading through the line of cars to get to his Mission Street exit ramp. A few minutes later, he pulled the Crown Vic into the driveway of his turn-of-the-century bungalow near the heart of the city, his jaw clenched so tight, it felt like his teeth would shatter. No, he couldn't ever forget.

He looked up at the house, all but oblivious to the peeling white paint on the wooden siding and the riot of unruly flowers surrounding the walkway. Taking a deep breath, he shoved open the car door and climbed out.

When he reached the house, he batted aside a climbing vine and pulled open the screen door. Inserting the key in the lock, he pushed through and entered. A gaunt, pale woman greeted him at the doorway, wrapped in a thick, worn quilt even though it was 80 degrees outside. Her large blue eyes, red-rimmed from constant tears, had dark hollows beneath them. Despite the air of pure despair that surrounded her, so sharp he felt it cutting into his own skin, she smiled weakly at him. "Hey, Billy," she said in a voice that sounded as if it hadn't been used in decades.

"Jenna," was all he could say in reply, as part of him begged her not to disappear. Again.

BACON. With a single-mindedness only the housebound possess, Maggie meticulously searched the contents of the freezer for bacon to go with the Cobb salad she'd just tossed. Shoving aside microwave dinners, plastic bags of vegetable medley and a box of frozen peach yogurt pops, she finally found the package of bacon and tossed it on the counter with a frozen clatter. She'd cook it up fresh, of course, because there was no way she'd have those horrible crumbled bits that came in a bottle and tasted like small shards of plastic.

For now, she ignored the package, carefully piling the frozen foods she'd displaced back into the freezer—TV dinners she had for lunch went on one side, and the packaged foods requiring more preparation on the other. Dessert boxes and vegetable bags went on top of the entire arrangement, since they were the least stable.

A faint, icy mist caressed her face, sending a chill down her entire body and raising goosebumps on her forearms, exposed by the rolled-up sleeves of her sweatshirt. She took her hand away, letting the freezer door fall shut.

So cold. That night in the swamp, so long ago. Naked, alone, and so cold. With only the sounds of cicadas and owls and the smell of the dank, fetid waters of the Atchafalaya to keep her company. Until he came back to the decaying cabin, with a sharp knife and the look of a starving man in his dark eyes— things she'd only read about in her books before that spring night. The chill had gotten worse while he studied her, his mouth forming the words that would haunt her long after that night: ''Why don't you run?'' *But that was the joke, with her hands and feet completely immobilized by fishing line, she couldn't run. Not even when he'd started cutting.*

She slammed the heavy frying pan she'd taken off the stove onto the counter, the force of the blow reverberating up her entire arm. Bacon, dammit.

A little bit of cooking spray. A dash of oil. Bacon.

She defrosted the package in the microwave, then peeled a few tepid slices off, tossing them into the pan with shaking hands. *Breathe, Maggie.* After adding a couple of extras in case Adriana wanted a salad when she came over with the week's supply of groceries, she turned on the stove burner. Bacon. She could do this. Bacon, bacon, bacon baconbaconbaconbacon...

Whump. Maggie whirled around at the sound, like a hand smacking the glass panes of one of the windows in the next room. Hard. Operating on pure instinct, she focused her senses on pinpointing the potential danger, only noticing that she was brandishing the frying pan over her head when she felt a slice of slimy, lukewarm meat slide down her arm. It fell to the floor with a soft smack and was soon followed by a larger clump. Warm oil slid down the pan and dribbled onto her hand and wrist.

The sound of laughter drew her gaze outside the bay windows. A young couple walked near the rocks by the ocean, tossing a tennis ball for their Irish setter, which scampered ahead of them, tongue lolling out of its mouth as a breeze blew back its shiny red coat. Grinning sheepishly, the man—a sandy blonde wearing a backward Angels cap and baggy shorts that went down to the middle of his tanned calves—held the ball in the air and shrugged apologetically at her.

"Maggie, you paranoid idiot," she muttered through her teeth, smiling back at him and raising the frying pan in salute. She deliberately relaxed her shoulders, feeling some of the tension leave her body while she watched the boy throw the ball again for the dog. His girlfriend ran to catch up with them and grabbed the brim of his cap, starting a laughing game of tag that continued until they were out of the range of Maggie's window.

She set the pan down on the counter with a wistful smile, noticing that her pulse had returned almost to normal. Or as normal as it had been since Billy Corrigan, the FBI agent with more than his share of mojo, had walked through her door.

The thought made her laugh as she turned off the stove, then pulled a clump of paper towels off the stand near the sink to clean up the mess on the floor. It really had been too long since she'd been on a date. At this rate, she'd be attacking the UPS man the next time he came over with a delivery. A disturbing image popped into her head of herself dressed in Saran Wrap, draping herself across poor Leonard Hobbes in his brown shorts and knee socks while she told him how much she loved a man in uni-foh-am.

She made a mental note to do a few extra miles on the treadmill that night.

The sound of the doorbell brought her out of her thoughts. With a hurried swipe, she picked up most of the bacon on the floor with her paper towels and deposited it in the stainless-steel trash can. After quickly washing her hands, she yanked the sunflower-patterned towel off the oven-door handle, drying her hands as she went to the door. One glance through the peephole told her Adriana had arrived.

When she pulled the door open, Adriana Torres

practically skidded inside, the panels of her red tartan miniskirt swirling around legs encased in black tights that were cut off at the ankles. She quickly dropped the groceries, snapping her gum nervously as she ran a hand through her caramel-brown hair, which was streaked with fire-engine-red highlights—temporary, Maggie hoped. Adriana owned a clothing resale boutique—Maggie knew better than to call it a thrift store—on Cannery Row in Monterey, and she had a tendency to look as though she'd just stepped out of a punk-rock musical.

"What's up?" Maggie asked, not yet sure whether to laugh at Addy's drama-queen tendencies or to sit her down and force her to spill whatever was bothering her.

With a whimper, Adriana lurched forward and enveloped Maggie in a surprisingly strong embrace for someone who couldn't have weighed more than 110 pounds wet. True confessions time it was, then. "What's going on?" Maggie asked, her hands curling upward as she adjusted to Addy's strong embrace. "You sound like you just sprinted down all of Seventeen Mile Drive."

"*Ay,* I'm just glad you're okay." Adriana leaned back and stared at her for a moment, then hugged her tightly again, cracking her gum with a vengeance.

"Of course I am," Maggie said, her voice calm and strong as she assumed the once-familiar role of caretaker in a crisis. "Why wouldn't I be? Girlfriend, you're scaring me."

Adriana put her hands briefly on Maggie's cheeks,

a "poor shut-in Magdalena" look on her face. Then she backed off, twisting the silver bangles on one wrist and muttering to herself in Spanish. One thing about Adriana—she'd been an American citizen for eighteen years, but her English, which was perfect in most circumstances, almost completely deserted her under stress. And if Maggie knew her correctly, she would mutter for a few more moments and then...après muttering, le déluge.

Addy didn't disappoint. She took a deep gulp of air and then let it rip. "Okay. First thing we have to do is call James. He'll know what to do. Then we have to get you over to my house somehow without your flipping over. Maybe with good drugs you can leave the state, even—"

"Flipping out," Maggie corrected her automatically. "Addy, breathe." She was dying to know what had gotten Adriana so spun up, but she knew she'd never find out if the woman passed out in her entryway.

"But—"

"Breathe."

Adriana threw her slender hands in the air, her rings sparkling under the skylight, and cursed rapidly in Spanish. "*Por el amor de Dios,* Magdalena Luz, I'm a yoga instructor. I know how to breathe." The yoga was a new thing. Addy taught classes after hours in the upstairs rooms of her shop in an effort to share her latest obsession with the world.

"Could've fooled me," Maggie responded. But when a film of water grew over Adriana's large green eyes, Maggie knew it was serious. "Addy, tell me what's going on," she said softly.

Adriana shook her head, a thin line of worry forming between her eyebrows.

Tension coiled like a tightly wound snake between Maggie's shoulders, and she felt the cold wrapping around her body once more. "Tell me."

"Go stand over there." Biting her lip, Adriana turned her slender body and swept a graceful arm toward the living room to her right. Maggie stepped around her and walked into the room, bracing herself for whatever was coming.

But you know what's coming, Maggie. You've known all along.

Grasping the brass handle, Adriana pulled the heavy wooden door open. From her vantage point, Maggie could see the door clearly, but her view outside was completely obscured. Then Adriana stepped back, and she could see only the door.

Someone had stabbed a long, serrated hunting knife in the center of the wood.

Chapter Four

Not a ghost, or a vision. Just a too-vivid memory that echoed in the stark halls of his empty home. He would have thought that the months would have eased the pain of Jenna's death, but every day, every damn day, Billy could see her and hear her as clearly as if she were actually standing before him. Everything but touch her.

"Jenna," he said again. And then his sister was gone.

This one had been from three years ago—her high-school prom. Biggest night of her life, up to that point, and she'd come down with food poisoning. She'd met him at the door, wrapped in an old quilt with a weak smile on her face. He'd helped her into bed, held her long, sand-colored hair while she was sick. He'd called her boyfriend Tom and apologized for her, then convinced her to stay in bed when she'd wanted to crawl to the Mission High School gym, bad breath and gray complexion be damned.

He'd thought there'd be a hundred more dates. A thousand more dances.

He shook his head with a sharp jerk, half wishing the violent movement would clear the images once and for all. But they were still there. They'd always be there. At least he could be thankful that the brutal slide-show memories of the crime-scene photos only assaulted him on special occasions.

Billy strode through the house he and Jenna had shared before she'd gone off to college. He went into the living room, tearing off his T-shirt and shedding the rest of his clothes as he went. Empty picture frames hung on the pale-green walls, the contents torn out and the glass long since swept away. As usual, he paid them no mind. Stripped down to his boxers, he picked up a pair of gray sweatpants that had been carelessly tossed over the back of a battered blue recliner and put them on. Some white athletic tape lay in the chair's seat cushion, and he scooped it up to wrap his hands. His slender hacker's hands with their wiry tendons and fingertip calluses from rapid typing. His good-for-nothing hands.

He'd destroyed most of the living room furniture long ago, other than the recliner and the TV set. The other half of the room was bare, except for the Everlast punching bag hanging from the ceiling by a thick metal chain. Billy figured it was probably the only thing standing between him and the deep well of insanity Maggie Reyes had fallen into.

Beautiful, crazy Maggie.

He punched with his right hand, then followed with a quick jab from his left. Right. Left. Uppercut. Jab.

Right. Left. Uppercut. Jab. He would not think of Maggie.

Controlling his breathing, he fell into the familiar rhythm of hard exercise for the next couple of hours. Small drops of sweat flicked off his hair and forehead with every movement, but he didn't stop to wipe his face. He didn't need to. After an hour or two of a punishing workout, he didn't feel much of anything. And that was the point.

Right. Left. Uppercut. Jab. Right. Left. Uppercut. Jab.

Jenna.

The next punch went wild and his fist skimmed off the bag, tipping him off balance, and he crashed to the floor. His right hip and elbow hit the bare wooden boards with a loud smack.

"Jesus," he breathed, unsure whether it was a curse or a prayer. He rolled over onto his back, his arms flung out from his sides as he caught his breath.

"Nope, just me," a voice said above him. "Not that I haven't been confused with the divine before."

Billy swiped the back of his hand across his eyes and pushed himself up into a sitting position. "Agent Parker," he said calmly, as if his boss wandered into his house uninvited every day.

"Special Agent Corrigan." Somewhere in that ageless territory between fifty and infinity, Fay Parker, Special Agent in Charge of the San Francisco field office, strode into the room and sat down on the edge of his recliner. She smoothed the skirt of her black power suit before crossing her ankles and fixing him with the stare that had earned her the nickname "the Basilisk." One slight move of her head, and her gold wire glasses slipped far enough down her nose so she could eye him over the rims. "You're a goddamn mess, Agent Corrigan," she said finally, her deep, raspy voice the hallmark of too many cigarettes.

Billy leaned back against the wall and drew his knees up so he could rest his elbows on them, only slightly breathless from the two hours he'd spent at the bag. "I am." He paused. "Ma'am."

She raised an eyebrow at the hint of challenge in his tone, but chose to ignore it. "Well, now that everyone's in agreement." Her voice was soft, but cold. "Judge Randall told me she hasn't seen hide nor hair of you or the affadavit for the DigiSystems case you told me you were going to submit today. Where is it? And where's the cell phone you're supposed to have with you at all times?" She tapped her fingers rapidly on the chair arm, but otherwise gave no outward sign of her agitation. But she was agitated.

"I'm sorry, Agent Parker," he said, not bothering to point out that he'd never been late with a paperwork at any other time in his career. Except when they'd called him about Jenna. "I thought it could wait until morning." The T-shirt he'd tossed away earlier lay next to him, and he grabbed it, using it to wipe his face before he put it on. "But my guess is you didn't come here for that, or to remind me to turn on my cell phone."

She didn't even blink. "Okay, Billy, then how

about you enlighten me as to why you were sniffing up Maggie Reyes's skirt this afternoon?''

Nothing the all-seeing Parker said should have surprised him, but he was still taken aback.

''Oh, yes, I know where you were today. I've been watching you for a long time.'' She took the glasses from her face and leaned forward, the thin line of her mouth softening slightly. ''I make it my business to know when one of my agents is about to sabotage the hell out of his career.''

He sat up a little straighter at her remark, feeling suddenly pinned down by her gaze.

''It's been two years, son. I know you never get over losing a family member, but you're killing yourself over this.''

He shook his head, but couldn't bring himself to form the words of denial that automatically rose to his lips.

''You work all the time. You cut off all contact with the people you used to see socially. You rarely talk to anyone outside of the job.'' She shrugged, a faint trace of pity in her dark eyes. ''Not that that's abnormal in a unit full of techno-geeks, but it's never been normal for you. Driving your body and mind to the brink of exhaustion every damn day for nearly two years is eventually going to take its toll.'' She folded her glasses into her fist with a small snap. ''And I don't want *any* of my agents in the field with you when you finally crack, Corrigan. This has to stop.''

He didn't even bother to ask her what. "He killed my sister. And he's coming here."

She lifted her eyebrows. "Says who? Certainly not Violent Crimes."

"Maggie."

"Oh, it's 'Maggie' now, is it?" Parker stood, her iron-gray bob swinging along her jawline with her sudden movement. "I don't care if the entire city of Monterey decides to throw a parade in the Surgeon's honor. This is not a case for the Computer Crimes Division. And, given your position in the Bureau, this is not a case for you."

Billy rose off the floor. Parker was only five foot six to his six-three, but she had the presence of an Amazon, and he wasn't about to let her loom over him. He hated people who loomed.

"I know what you want, Corrigan, and I'm warning you now, I will not have vigilante justice in my department. I'll say it again." She punctuated her words by shaking her glasses at him. "This. Is. Not. Your. Case."

Billy relaxed his stance, as if in preparation for physical combat rather than a battle of wills. "Jenna was everything I had," he said quietly. "I won't stop looking for him. You can fire me now, if you have to, but I won't ever stop."

She didn't even blink. "Turn in your badge and your gun."

Without hesitation, Billy walked to where his jeans lay on the floor and took his badge wallet out of one of the pockets. His gun rested on the fireplace mantle, and he picked that up, too, then handed both items to her.

The room grew quiet for several seconds as they stared at each other. Parker was the first to crack. "Damn you, you stupid, stubborn male." She sighed and shook her head. "This is an extended leave of absence. When you're ready to give up any and all delusions that you're John Wayne, give me a call."

She placed the items he'd given her onto the recliner she'd just vacated. "Now. Promise me one thing, Corrigan," she said.

"If I can," he answered.

"If, through some giant stroke of luck, you run into that son of a bitch before the Violent Crimes Division does, you follow the law to the letter. Because if I hear just a hint of the words *excessive force* in a sentence with your name in it, I will not lift a finger to save you."

She spun around and walked to the door, then stopped just before exiting. "Live, Billy," she said. "Please, just live."

MAGGIE'S VISION CLOUDED and tunneled until all she could see was the vicious hunting knife, the serrated teeth on its top edge tearing into the wood on her door. She remembered that knife. The Surgeon had worn a mask when he'd taken her, and she'd never seen his face, but she'd remember that knife for the rest of her days. Every time she looked at the scars on her stomach.

"Addy, get a plastic bag from the kitchen, would

you?'' Her own voice sounded tinny and remote to her ears. She didn't notice Adriana leave the room, but suddenly, the plastic bag was in her hand. She wrapped it around her fingers and pulled the knife out of her door. A piece of paper fluttered to the floor.

Then her vision cleared, widened, and she could see beyond the door, outside, down her sand-strewn driveway to the copse of trees across the street, so thick she wouldn't know if someone were standing among them right now, watching.

The tremors were small, at first, starting with her fingers and vibrating up her arms, but soon, her entire body was shaking and jerking hard enough to make her teeth chatter. Her hand loosened its grip on the knife and it clattered to the floor, but still she stood in the open doorway as if rooted to the spot. Staring at the trees.

Adriana gripped her shoulders and steered her toward the couch. She pushed a glass of water in Maggie's hands before moving away to shut the door. She was saying something, or her mouth was moving anyway, but Maggie had no idea what was coming out. She barely managed to catch the words "—calling 911.''

He'd been at her doorstep. In the trees outside her home. And all she could do was stay holed up in her house like the proverbial sitting duck, practically inviting him to come inside and finish what he'd started. She glanced at the thin panes of glass that separated her from the Surgeon's terrible hands. How had she ever thought this house, that glass, could keep her safe when it would shatter so easily?

"Little pig, little pig, let me come in…"

Oh, no.

She stood up and backed away from the window.

"…Maggie? Maggie, please."

Maggie glanced down at the hand on her arm. Focused on the thin silver rings and graceful fingers. Focus. She had to focus.

"Maggie, James *esta aqui*. I have answered most of his questions but you have to talk to him, *por favor*." Adriana's voice brought her out of her thoughts. "Please?"

She shook her head, scrubbed her hand over her eyes. She'd obviously been in la-la land for some time, it didn't seem like enough time had passed for the police to be here already. "Sure, Addy. Of course I'll talk to him." She tightened her mouth upward in what she hoped was a smile and looked around until she zeroed in on the real James Brentwood, a tall, brown-haired man in a rumpled shirt and tie, bouncing up and down on the balls of his feet. He wore a pair of trendy brown glasses, behind which were sparkling brown eyes, set deeply in a face that seemed to crinkle into a smile naturally. There was an almost frenetic energy about him—even his hair cowlicked wildly about his head, as if it, too, couldn't stand still. "Hello, Detective Brentwood," she said, putting on her best I'm-a-sane-productive-member-of-society voice.

He reached forward and clasped her hand in his in

a brief handshake. "Maggie Reyes. A pleasure."
Brentwood introduced her to his partner, Detective
Elizabeth Borkowski—Billy's friend, she noted—
who had gathered up the knife and the note in plastic
bags. Borkowski was a petite brunette with short,
curly hair, milk-white skin dotted with pale freckles,
and a wedding ring on her left hand.

Borkowski quickly excused herself and headed outside to check the yard and exterior of the house. Maggie gestured for Brentwood to have a seat. He sank
down into the overstuffed, sage-green sofa in the living room and had a brief battle of wills and elbows
with the throw pillows piled up near the armrest.
When they'd been beaten into submission, Brentwood
leaned back and settled in. Adriana lowered herself
next to him.

"So," Brentwood began after they'd dispensed
with the kind of pleasantries that usually made Maggie irritable. This time, however, they were a welcome delay of the inevitable. She really didn't want
to think about what that knife or that note meant just
now.

But obviously, Brentwood wasn't going to give her
the reprieve she was craving. He placed the note,
bagged in plastic, on the table and shoved it toward
her. "Any idea what this means?" Sitting back, he
batted his too-long brown hair out of his eyes.

She scanned the letter that had been impaled to her
door moments before. Someone had scrawled *Do you
want to live forever?* in heavy, uneven letters. Underneath was scribbled, *S10 M0*. Seemingly meaning-

less, but if she knew the Surgeon, the message was just as important as the words she knew well.

As soon as she saw the three men in black come through the door of the rotting cabin, she instinctively jerked against her bonds, the movement nearly exhausting what remained of her strength. A sharp pain shot through her wrists as the fishing line cut into her skin, and then she could feel something wet dripping down her arms. Her mind felt thick, ponderous, and it took her a few moments to comprehend that her wrists were bleeding.

She blinked, her eyelids closing and opening in the slowest of motions, and the three men before her coalesced into one. One man, with a neoprene ski mask on his face and a nylon stocking over his hair. One man with a starving, frenzied look in his too-bright eyes.

The springs of the rusty cot creaked as he climbed on top of her, and she heard the sound of metal sing against leather. Slowly, ponderously, she turned her head and saw the large hunting knife he held next to her cheek. With one hand, he looped a leather cord around her neck; the other brought the tip of the knife to the hollow in her throat.

"Do you wanna live forever, Maggie?" he whispered, and he trailed the knife down her breastbone, leaving a thin red line in its wake.

Lost in her thoughts, Maggie barely noticed as her hands jerked upward to clutch at her throat. At the sudden movement, Adriana sprang up from her perch on the sofa arm. "Maggie?" she said.

Maggie shook her head, coming fully back to the present. She waved her friend off with an apologetic smile. "That question—" She picked up the bagged note Brentwood had passed to her and tapped its shiny surface with a fingernail. "—was something the Surgeon asked me when—" She swallowed, trying desperately not to remember any more. "That night." She trusted that Brentwood would know exactly what night she was referring to.

He did. He took off his tortoiseshell glasses and chewed on one of the bows while his right leg bobbed up and down like a sewing-machine needle. "You think he's followed you from Louisiana to Monterey." It was a statement, not a question, but she nodded anyway.

"I know how that sounds," she said, handing the note back to him. It sounded crazy, that's how it sounded. She knew it; he knew it.

James nodded grimly. "Serial killers don't normally stalk across long distances. Especially not after a victim has gone into hiding." His brow was furrowed in a look of concerned understanding laced with pity. He didn't believe her.

"I'm no ordinary victim," Maggie responded.

"You think he's following you because of your books?" James asked.

Maggie had to admire the man. By now, most people would have passed into the "you flaming idiot" phase of the conversation. "In the criminal world, I'm something of a celebrity. You want to live forever? Just have Maggie Reyes write your story." She got up and paced to the fireplace, focusing her attention on a photo of herself and her parents that rested on the mantle. She didn't remember when it had been taken, but it must have been years ago; they were outdoors. Not to mention she hadn't seen them for eighteen months.

"What you're talking about is uncharted territory." James said behind her. "According to the feds, the Surgeon is your basic organized lust killer. He's smart enough to plan and cover his tracks, but he kills from compulsion."

"No killer cannibalized his victims with the enthusiasm Jeffrey Dahmer had. No one put up a better guise of sanity than Ted Bundy. No one broke more of the profilers 'rules' than the DC snipers." Maggie turned to face him. "They're *all* uncharted territory, Detective Brentwood. And no one has ever tracked victims with the single-mindedness of the Surgeon."

"So he's communicating with you so you'll write a book about him?"

Ah-ha. Now she was getting polite disbelief. Time to bring out the big guns. "The woman who was killed in Carmel—Abigail Rhodes. Did that look like an ordinary murder to you?"

Brentwood put his glasses back on his face and pushed them as far up his nose as they would go. His leg continued to keep time to some rhythm only he could sense. "I'm not at liberty to discuss—"

"Abigail had reported harassing phone calls to the police three days prior to her death," Maggie broke in, recounting what she knew of the case. "The night of the murder, someone broke into her apartment. There was no sign of forced entry. She was quickly incapacitated by a blow to the head, then tied to her bed and stabbed repeatedly in an almost ritualistic fashion. You found no fingerprints, few fibers, and nothing that would let you point to a particular suspect with any certainty.''

James cleared his throat. ''That was all in the papers,'' he began, his manner still unfailingly polite.

''And here's what wasn't.'' Moving quickly across the room, she sat on the edge of the chair across from him, the coffee table between them. ''He used fishing line to tie her wrists and ankles. She was strangled, but that's not what killed her. The cause of death was heavy blood loss due to several cuts on her abdomen arranged in a particular pattern resembling a grid.''

The detective's leg stopped bouncing.

''Oh, and one more thing,'' Maggie said. ''He took something off her body—like a piece of jewelry or a scrap of clothing. It's his trophy, Detective Brentwood. He'll touch it and look at it and relive his crime over and over and over again. And when reliving it isn't enough, he'll find some other young woman and he'll do the same thing all over again. Unless you're there to stop him.''

Her macabre litany finished, Maggie sat back against the soft upholstery of the chair, feeling strangely tired. Ever since she'd read about Abigail Rhodes, she'd been so damn tired.

The detective stared at her for a long moment, then

steepled his hands and brought them to his lips, resting his thumbs under his square chin.

"I told you she knew what she was talking about," Adriana said behind him.

"Why is he so fixated on you? Will he come here?" the man finally said.

"Eventually," Maggie replied. "He'll kill me because he wants immortality."

"Right," James said. "Kill the woman who immortalized the Green River Killer, the Zodiac murders, Mohammed and Malvo, and you'd have yourself a hell of a biography."

The three of them grew suddenly quiet, remaining motionless until Adriana started fishing inside her purse. The sound of crinkling wrappers broke the silence, and then Addy shoved a piece of gum in her mouth and began snapping away. She tossed the pack on the table. "Nerves," she explained. "Help yourselves."

James patted her knee gently and then turned his focus back to Maggie. "What about these letters and numbers?"

"I think he might be keeping score," she replied. "Ten murders for him, no leads for me. In New Orleans, I was on the task force that was trying to catch him."

"Hmmm." Brentwood turned the note over. "And this?"

Taped to the back was a photo. Maggie stepped closer, too intrigued to be frightened yet by the picture she hadn't known was there. She picked up the bag and examined its contents. The photo was severely out of focus; the only thing she could tell was that it was taken inside a room with generic beige walls, and the subject was a woman with curly black hair.

"Maggie?" Brentwood's voice broke her concentration.

"Well, that's new." She licked her lips. "He's definitely sending a message." She put the note down and pulled the rubber band off the end of her braid, combing her fingers through her hair until her black curls cascaded freely over her shoulders. From the look on Brentwood's face, it was clear he knew what she was going to say next. "I think that's me."

Brentwood narrowed his eyes and squinted at the photo. "You don't recognize anything in the background, do you?"

She shook her head. "That beige wall could be anywhere. This house, my home in New Orleans, any one of the places I used to give lectures." She gave him a small smile. "Unfortunately, I've always had huge hair, so I couldn't even tell you when this was taken. Especially since the face is so out of focus."

Brentwood continued asking questions, and she answered, doing her best to keep herself divorced from the reality that was coming out of her mouth. Finally, the questions stopped, and he simply looked at her, with Adriana cracking her gum on the couch next to him. Brentwood's mouth flattened, and he clenched his jaw tightly. The man wouldn't have made a very good poker player.

"You can't do anything," she said. "I know."

He stood, played with his tie, though his eyes never left hers. If he had to leave her at the mercy of a madman, at least he'd be honest and forthright about it. "It could be a prank. A lot of kids in this area know about your...condition."

The crazy woman on Mermaid Point. Oh, yeah, they knew all right. "Sure," she said.

"Even if he were stalking you, serial killers normally don't stray from their comfort zones. This would be highly unusual."

"Right." Her gaze traveled out the window, to the shadows between the trees across the street.

"We'll check for fingerprints on the knife and the note. If it's any of our known offenders—"

"You won't find anything," Maggie interrupted flatly. "He's better than that."

Adriana, who'd been listening carefully to the entire exchange, finally burst out, "James, can't you do something? What if she's really not safe?"

"I'll arrange for extra patrols past your house." He shoved his hands in his pockets, then pulled them out again. "I'm sorry, it's all I can do at this point."

I'm sorry. I'm sorry. How many people had been apologizing to her lately? Would they keep saying it, even if she were dead? "Thank you. I appreciate it."

He shoved his hands in the pockets of his tan trenchcoat, looking a little as if he ought to be in a black-and-white noir film. "I'm listening, Maggie. Call me if you have anything else." Then he turned to leave.

Maggie turned and walked into the kitchen, only half listening to Adriana argue with Brentwood as she went outside to see him to his car.

She traced her fingers around the smooth, cool lid of her blue sugar canister, the Firestar nestled inside once more, loaded and ready. There were other weapons hidden around the house—guns, knives, Mace. Would they be enough?

They had to be.

Last time around, she'd had the protection of the entire NOPD and a few FBI agents, and it hadn't been enough. She'd had her gun, her martial arts training, her normally flawless intuition that had warned her of approaching danger countless times. None of it had kept her safe.

Now, she had what her former colleagues politely called ''a psychological condition,'' she jumped at mere shadows, and she had all the credibility of an alcoholic bag lady. Sure, her friends and family would be there for her if she asked, but she couldn't involve them. Keeping them far away from this crazy game, more than anything, had to be her first priority. This time, despite the fact that Addy's detective might believe her, she was alone.

Her eyes fell on Billy Corrigan's card.

She palmed it off the table, then curled her fingers around it until it was crushed inside her fist.

All alone.

Chapter Five

Maggie balanced her weight evenly on the soles of both feet and slowly raised her arms upward to greet the sky—well, in her case, the ceiling. Tadasana—mountain pose. Adriana had told her that the yoga posture improved alignment, balance, confidence, and was good for people who constantly felt cold.

So far, it wasn't helping with any of it.

She exhaled and bent her body at the waist, dropping her hands in front of her until her fingertips swept the ground. Shifting the bulk of her weight to her palms, she pushed one leg backward into a lunge, then brought the other leg back to meet it. Plank pose. The second part of a sequence that was supposed to "invigorate the nervous system" and relax her.

Whatever.

Do you wanna live forever, Maggie?

The whisper was so real, Maggie could almost feel the Surgeon's breath on her cheek, the tingling steel of the knife blade as he trailed it down her spine with soft, butterfly touches that would soon turn vicious.

Her arms gave out and she landed hard on her stomach. One breath. Two.

How would she ever stop him this time? Closing her eyes, she dropped her head forward until her forehead touched the soft surface of her yoga mat. Her hands curled around her face, creating a barrier that blocked her peripheral vision and reduced her world to one small square of blue foam. One breath. Two.

If you run, he can't getcha. If you run, he can't getcha. If yourunhecan'tifyourunifyourunifyourun....

"I can't," she moaned, a small pathetic noise from a small, pathetic person. "I can't."

A loud banging noise echoed through the house, abruptly bringing an end to her latest mental mini-collapse. The front door.

Maggie closed her eyes and listened to the muffled sound of the waves hitting the beach for a moment. Thank heaven for this house near the ocean—water always managed to relax her when she needed it most. Even through a barrier of stucco walls and thick panes of glass.

The banging on her door grew louder and more insistent. With a sigh, Maggie slowly rose to her feet, bringing her hands to the ceiling to stretch her spine one last time. Then, she pulled the coated rubber band out of her hair and quickly finger-combed it before redoing her ponytail. No sense looking like a crazy person, even if it was probably just Adriana kicking the door because she held a bag of groceries in her hands.

With one hand on the wall for balance, Maggie

started to rise on her tiptoes to look through the peep-hole, but then dropped back down. She reached out and clamped her fingers around the small yellow spray can that sat on the nearby phone table. Just in case.

When she did glance through the peephole, what she saw made her wish she hadn't bothered inter-rupting a perfectly good nervous breakdown. "I have Mace," she called through the wood.

"It's important," came Billy Corrigan's muffled reply.

She didn't answer, preferring instead to remain quiet and see how long it took him to give up and go away. But instead of walking to the other side of the house, she stayed in place, watching him through the small bit of magnifying glass. Today his T-shirt was plain gray, and his jeans were the dark, smoky blue her Abercrombie & Fitch catalog called "dirty wash." Trendy guy.

Maggie turned around abruptly and leaned her back against the door, folding her arms and making a men-tal note to avoid scrutinizing Billy Corrigan's ward-robe or any other part of him. Then again, since she wasn't about to open the door, she probably wouldn't have the chance. He'd probably leave for good if she could just keep him out this one time—out of her home, out of danger, out of her life, so she wouldn't be tempted to make the mistake of depending on the FBI to save her. Because that had worked so *well* the last time around....

"Agent Corrigan, do you have a subpoena?" she called through the barrier between them.

Pause. "No."

"Then I am not required by law to open this door or talk to you?"

"Maggie—"

"Right then. Off you go." With that, she finally managed to make herself walk away, ignoring the fact that part of her was dying to let gray-eyed Billy Corrigan inside.

OUTSIDE, BILLY SMACKED his palm against the pale stucco exterior of Maggie's house. What would it take for her to open the damn door and let him in? Why couldn't he find the right words, for once? Just this once, when it really mattered?

"Do you know what day tomorrow is?" he called. Then he waited.

Nothing. Not even the mention of October 8th got a response.

"It's an anniversary, Maggie. Two years ago tomorrow, the Surgeon killed his first victim in New Orleans."

This time, he waited for what felt like half the afternoon, but still Maggie refused to open the door. He pressed his ear to the wood, and the silence that greeted him made him wonder if she hadn't walked out of earshot, into the depths of her house.

He pushed away from the door, nearly growling in frustration. "Dammit, Maggie, people are going to die. Doesn't anyone matter to you anymore?"

Abruptly, the door swung open, and then Maggie stood before him with eyes that had changed from brown to angry black since the last time he'd seen her.

"Matter? How can you ask me that? Of course they matter." She jabbed her index finger at him, stopping just short of poking him sharply in the chest. "Janine Black, age 27. Long brown hair, green eyes, height, five-seven. Poli-sci major at Tulane University with minors in theater and social services. Abducted from campus while walking back to her dorm from rehearsing *My Fair Lady,* where she was playing Eliza Doolittle. Her body was found behind a church in Metairie. She left behind her parents and one younger sister, none of whom have even begun to recover from her death." Blinking back tears, she tapped her left index finger with her right. "Tess Hartshorn, age 24. She was killed in an alley near the Magnolia Café, where she worked as a waitress while putting herself through UNO's MBA program. She had a baby son she was trying to raise while the no-good father spent most of his time gambling on the waterfront." She ticked off another finger. "Carrie Stern was an accountant at Foster, Jones and Hyde. She liked making jewelry. Morgan Anderson was a research intern at University Hospital with a thing for frogs and the color purple. They all matter." Maggie paused to look down at her fingers, maybe considering, as he was, what poor substitutes they made for the lives they represented. She didn't say the name, but he knew it was there. Hanging between them, ready to slam him in the solar plexus the minute it fell from her lips. Jenna.

There were some things about his sister that Billy hadn't wanted to know. He'd seen the crime scene photos, read the files and newspaper articles he'd had to read, but there were some questions he just hadn't wanted to know the answers to.

How long had it taken? Had the rohypnol worn off before she died? Could she feel the knife? Had she suffered? Did she cry?

Could he ever, *ever* pay enough for not being there to save her?

Maggie touched him then, just a flutter of her fingertips against his arm, bare under the short sleeve of his T-shirt. He focused on her face, and it brought him back, away from the thoughts that would make him crazier than she was reputed to be. Her touch made him sane again, just for a moment.

"Maggie," he rasped, his voice dangerously close to breaking point. Like the rest of him.

"I can't help you, Billy," she said softly. "God, I wish I could."

He didn't respond. He couldn't. Vengeance was the only thing keeping him alive, now that everyone that had ever mattered to him was gone. He couldn't do it alone, couldn't break the law any more than he already had without jeopardizing any chance he had of catching the Surgeon. She was his only chance, she and the vestiges of a once-brilliant mind that could fill in the missing pieces of the puzzle before him. She could bring him the only solace he'd ever find in this life after Jenna's murder. He wanted to tell her how he'd thought of crushing the life out of the man who'd killed his sister, in gross, exacting detail. He wanted to tell her how lost he felt without his family, how bewildered and angry that he was the only one of them left in this world. He wanted to tell her all of it, but he could only stare at her, feeling like a drowning man. So much to say, and he couldn't find the right words.

"Help me," he managed finally.

"Don't do this, Billy," she said, her expression softer, not angry anymore. "He'll take everything from you."

He almost laughed at that one. The words sliced through him with a sharp, raw pain he hadn't thought he could feel anymore. "Too late."

Maggie shook her head, the fountain of curls in her ponytail tumbling with the movement. "No, you could still—" She stopped suddenly, her gaze dropping to where her feet stood just beyond the threshold of the house.

Too late, he realized that she was standing in her open doorway, and that he was the only thing between her and the outdoors. He'd shifted. She'd noticed.

She inhaled sharply, suddenly, making a small "eeee" noise. Her eyes flicked over his shoulder and beyond, to the trees. "You could still...." She gasped, bringing a palm to her chest, just under her throat. Took another noisy breath, and another, faster and faster, until her respirations had the cadence of a speeding train. Her eyes grew wild and opened so wide, he could see a rim of white all around her pupils. With a jerky movement, she doubled over, her hands scrabbling at her throat.

Moving fast, Billy stepped forward and caught her in his arms. He lifted her off her feet and cradled her tightly against his chest, as if he could block what haunted her with his physical presence. He strode with her through the doorway, stopping only to kick the door closed behind him, and carried her into the living room. The sounds she was making were louder and more urgent, and though her eyes were right on his face, he knew she didn't see him.

Dammit, Maggie, what did he do to you?

"Come on, Maggie, slow down," he said, laying her gently on the couch and crouching beside her. She battered his body with flailing arms that pushed away at something he couldn't see. He ignored her blows and framed her small, deathly pale face with his large hands. Her breathing was still too rapid, too ragged. "Look at me, Maggie. Look at me."

Maggie blinked rapidly and turned her dilated gaze to meet his. Abruptly, she gripped his wrists with both of her hands and held on tight while the air ripped through her lungs. Inoutinoutinoutinoutinoutinout....

"Slowly, Maggie, come on," he said, using all his control to keep his voice soft and even. "Slow down. Look at me."

Her nails dug into his skin, drawing blood. He didn't care. "Just look at me. I've got you," he said, still cupping her face while she fought to control her ragged gasping. She clung to him and he did his best to hold her steady.

After an eternity, her breaths slowed to the rapid puffs of someone who'd just finished a 200-yard sprint. "That's it," he encouraged, taking his hand from her cheek to skim it along her hairline, down her jaw. He caught one of the loose curls that framed her face and let it run between his fingers. "That's great. You're doing great."

"I'm…s-sorry," she whispered between gasps.

"Don't," he replied. "Breathe."

"Too sc—…scared."

"I know."

She sucked in a shaky breath, held it, and then blew it back out in a rush. Inhaled again, held it. The pattern continued, until finally, he noted with crazy relief, the crisis seemed to have passed. She loosened her grip on his wrists, her fingers smoothing over the small, red half-moon marks her nails had made.

"I don't know if I can help you," she said finally, her voice stronger, though marred by the occasional shuddering inhalation.

"It doesn't matter," he said. She looked wiped out, so he helped her lie back on the couch.

"I know it does."

Picking up a quilt that lay across one of the armchairs, he shook out the folds and tucked it around her thin body.

She curled her hand around it and pulled the covering under her chin. Her eyes drifted shut, and she shifted until her body sank deeper into the couch cushions. "I'm so sorry you had to—"

"I don't mind." He sat down next to her, watching her with a familiar peacefulness he hadn't felt since Jenna had left for college. He watched her features relax and felt the tension leave his own shoulders as he listened to her breathing fall into a quiet, comfortable rhythm. Not Jenna. Something different.

"You don't have to stay," she murmured after a few moments.

"I'm not going anywhere."

A small smile drifted across her face. "You know something?"

"What's that?" he asked, almost smiling in return at how soft she was when nearly sleeping.

"When you're crazy, people don't touch you anymore," she said.

The hand clutching the blanket relaxed, and she slept.

WHEN MAGGIE woke a few hours later, the last thing she expected to see was Billy Corrigan asleep in the chair-and-a-half in her living room. But there he was, snoring away when she would have bet her shiny new laptop he'd run away after the little show she'd put on that afternoon.

"People don't touch you anymore," she muttered under her breath as she untangled herself from the blanket that had been wrapped around her. "Could I be any more of a sap?"

"I didn't mind," a deep voice said from the recliner, making Maggie jump. She was grateful it was nighttime, so he couldn't see the hot blush staining her cheeks.

"Uh, actually, if we could just forget that ever happened, I'd be grateful," she responded. The comment was met with silence, which obviously indicated Billy wasn't about to promise any such thing. Her not-so-finest moment would live on inside his head for a long time. Lovely.

"Do you always do that?" he asked.

"Do what?"

"Hide behind that smart mouth of yours?"

"Ahhh—" For the second time that night, she felt her face heat up. "You know, playing Let's Psychoanalyze Maggie isn't my favorite thing in the world. Do you mind if I change the subject?"

"No problem." She could hear a faint trace of laughter in his deep voice.

"What are you still doing here?" she asked.

"I didn't think you should wake up alone," he said.

There were so many ways to take that statement. She grabbed a corner of the blanket that now lay bunched to one side of the sofa and twisted it in her hands. "You came here this afternoon for a reason. What did you want?"

"Your help," he said.

She squinted, trying to make out the shape in the dark across from her. But the only light in the room came from the half moon outside the window as it ducked in and out of the cloud cover, so she couldn't see much more than shadows. "Why me?"

"You're outside law enforcement, and you probably know the Surgeon better than anyone." He paused. "And I can't go through regular FBI channels."

"Because you're in Computer Crimes," she responded, piecing his story together in her head. "You shouldn't be anywhere near this case. Especially since it hits so close to home."

"Something like that."

His voice was completely without inflection as he talked about the Surgeon, as if the thing that had killed his sister had bled all emotion from him in the process. "You don't want to bring this guy to justice. You want to kill him," she said, the pieces all falling into place.

"Something like that," he repeated.

Something told Maggie she couldn't have been further from her goal of persuading Billy Corrigan to leave her and the Surgeon's case alone. "Vigilante justice," she said into the dark. "What does your family think about that?"

"I don't have a family."

The words he'd spoken earlier came back to her, when she'd begged him to leave before the Surgeon took everything from him. *Too late.*

Did she really want to know that much about the stranger next to her? Did she dare ask? The question came out before she could stop herself, even though she knew better. "What happened, Billy?"

The shadow in the chair shifted, sighed. "Our parents died when she was twelve and I was nineteen. They were island-hopping in Hawaii on a puddle-jumper. Freak storm."

Plane crash. They'd been so young. Her parents were still alive, and their love and affection had always been apparent from her first memories until the present. She couldn't even wrap her mind around what Billy and Jenna Corrigan must've gone through. "How did you get custody of Jenna?"

He responded with a question of his own. "Ever heard of Interceptor?"

"The new computer program the FBI uses to scan e-mail and Internet correspondence for terrorist activity, not to mention violate the civil rights of every American who uses the Net?" she asked dryly. "Sure, I've heard of it."

"It's mine."

"What, you bought it?" she asked, confused. "You run it for the Bureau? What does that mean, 'it's mine?'"

"I built it."

"You—" The sheer enormity of what he'd just told her hit her so suddenly, she couldn't finish her sentence. She sat back against the overstuffed cushions of the sofa and absorbed what he'd just told her. Holy computer geek, Billy Corrigan was a bona fide genius. Who happened to be built like a brick house.

"I meant to destroy it," he said. "In the wrong hands, it's more than a tool for civil rights abuses."

"So why create it in the first place?"

The moon broke through the clouds and illuminated half of his face in blue light, sharpening the angles of his cheekbones and casting shadows in the hollows of his eyes. "I was young. Stupid. I did things like that all the time, just because I could."

Understanding dawned. "You were a hacker. And a really good one, at that." She thought of the money the FBI must've paid him for exclusive rights to Interceptor. Enough to make him a millionaire a hundred times over, she'd bet. Enough to hire the best child custody lawyers Social Services had ever come up against. "So you sold Interceptor to the FBI...."

"I would've sold my soul to keep my sister." The emptiness in his voice chilled her. Now his sister was dead, and everyone who'd ever loved him had been wiped off the face of the Earth. And Billy himself was probably so far gone, nothing but the Surgeon's death was going to bring him back. The moon ducked back under the clouds, and once again they were bathed in near-total darkness.

Now it all made sense—the earring in his left ear, the unconventional clothes, the way he bent the rules to win her trust. He was brilliant, and the FBI couldn't afford to lose him, even if he had less-than-professional bearing. And now he never would have it, because it was more than apparent that Billy Corrigan cared about only one thing—revenge.

Could she help him? Maggie didn't think so. She barely trusted herself anymore since the day she'd escaped from a cabin in the Atchafalaya. Sometimes, her mind felt like a moth-eaten piece of lace, held together only by slim threads of memory and mere vestiges of sanity. Could she pull it together one last time? Could she do more than sit in her house and be a victim? Could she possibly make a difference again, save someone's sister, friend, wife from Jenna Corrigan's fate?

She might not trust herself, but she trusted the FBI even less when it came to protecting her. The Surgeon had taken her from right under their noses in New Orleans. But Billy Corrigan was something new. Unconventional. Driven. Maybe by aligning herself with this rebellious genius, she could actually get one step ahead of the killer who had eluded state and federal law enforcement for over two years.

What if he gets too close? a nagging voice inside her head asked. The thought made her reach up and turn on the ironwork lamp standing next to the sofa. Billy didn't even blink at the sudden warm glow of the 110-watt lightbulb. His eyes were hollow, cold and so full of vengeance he couldn't even see her.

And suddenly, she knew what she had to do. No one should have to lose everyone they ever loved. No one. And even if the hope that the two of them could stop the grisly murders was an illusion, maybe by trying they could both come back to the living again. She didn't want to care about him, this sad, hollow stranger, but maybe that, too, was out of her control.

"He'll strike again, maybe even tomorrow." October 8th, the anniversary of his first kill in New Orleans. Her decision made, Maggie stood, the blanket that had been bunched on her lap puddling at her feet.

"I just hope that if we don't make any noise, he'll let this anniversary slide on by."

A GOOD SOLDIER doesn't just know patience, he *is* patience. A good soldier can wait for days without food, without sleep, without rest.

He waited, standing at attention in the shadows near the enemy's domicile, breathing in the pungent odor of the neoprene mask he wore to conceal himself. *Stand down, soldier. It is not yet time.*

The enemy moved about the kitchen area of her domicile, his presence undetected. Or maybe not. Maybe she knew he was there and her seemingly mundane actions were a way of taunting him. *You've been a bad, bad boy. Sinful, ungrateful son.*

He ripped the knife strapped to his thigh out of its scabbard, the metal blade singing against the leather. He looked around, to make sure no one had heard the music the knife made when he brought it out. He should have held still, been patient, but he often allowed himself this one luxury while standing watch.

The enemy opened a cupboard door, stretching her thin, lithe frame to reach something lodged on a top shelf. Her shirt rode up, and he could see the smooth skin of her lower back. *Sinful, shameful, dirty girl.* The enemy thought she could tempt him with the ways of the flesh.

The enemy was wrong.

He would purge her of her sin, make her pure as a newborn baby. But only when it was time. A good soldier knew all about time, how to wait, until the moment was perfect.

And then the sin would be washed away, and the enemy would be clean.

He wasn't supposed to enjoy the kill. A good soldier didn't. But that was his sin, one he carried with him all the time. Some days, he forgot all about the sin, as if it had shrunk to the size of a small pebble and lodged itself in a forgotten pocket of his mind. And then, on the days that he thought of as red days, that sin would grow, larger and larger, until he thought it would burst inside him and make his head explode. And then, on the red days, he would hunt the enemy, stalk her patiently, for as long as it took.

When they finally did meet, predator and prey, he would lose himself in her, in the blessed act of purging her of her sin, and then his own sin would be washed away.

He brought the knife to his mouth and licked the blade with a slow, deliberate movement of his tongue. It was almost time.

FUMBLING WITH HER KEYS, Gina Markson finally managed to insert the correct one into the deadbolt lock of the small cottage-style house—no small feat given that she held an overstuffed paper Winn-Dixie bag in each arm. But if she balanced one on her knee just right, she could always manage to unlock her door without putting them down.

And with her roommate Kelli's birthday party happening at precisely five o'clock tomorrow afternoon,

Gina needed every last second to get everything ready while writing a paper on the inherent misogyny of the metaphysical poets and managing to squeeze in a little time for her boyfriend Max.

Shoving the door open with her hip, Gina stumbled into the dark apartment and immediately threw the heavy bags on the kitchen counter. Her clunky black boot heels thumped on the hardwood floor as she lurched forward to fumble for the light switch over the sink.

There. Her hand found the switch and flicked it upward, and she felt ridiculously grateful when the light flooded the kitchen. She'd always hated the dark.

No particular reason why, other than the same old bogeymen that hid under beds and in closets and scared every small child to pieces. But unlike *normal* people, the fear of the dark had stayed with her. She was such a dork. She'd almost talked Kelli out of renting the place—despite the fact that it was minutes from grad school and had excellent walk-in closets— just because you actually had to walk to the other side of the kitchen to turn on the light after entering the front door. Not a fun thing at night.

But it was a small price to pay for the great location and noticeable lack of roaches. Her first house. Gina reached into one of the bags on the counter and started separating the contents into those things that needed to be put away, and those she would use for Kelli's birthday double-chocolate-fudge-decadence cookies. Some people liked cake on their birthdays; Kelli preferred cookies. This year, she'd get twenty-two.

"Eggs, butter, sugar, vanilla—pure, not imitation," she murmured to herself, remembering her mother's directions. The cookies had been her favorite growing up, and she knew they'd be perfect for the party tomorrow.

She sensed, rather than saw, the shadow dart behind her.

Gina whirled around, still clutching a carton of eggs. She scanned the dining area, her eyes darting quickly to the dim space under the battered antique dining table and around each of the three mismatched chairs. Nothing.

Freak, she admonished herself.

Straightening her spine, she put the eggs on the counter and walked through the kitchen to the living room entrance—the front of the apartment was L-shaped, so the living room hooked sharply off the right. With a movement she could only describe as spastic, she smacked her hand against the wall and quickly felt around until she hit the light switch. The overhead bulbs—covered by a large, glass dome with brass fixtures that Max once said looked suspiciously like a breast, the perv—cast a warm, yellow glow over Kelli's gray couch and Gina's wicker Pier One chair. Satisfied once that intrepid exploration yielded no intruders, Gina returned to her cookies. The extra light from the other room bled into the kitchen, she noticed, making her feel better about being in the house alone.

She opened one of the cupboards, taking out the Hello, Kitty! recipe box. A quick rifle through the handful of cards inside was all it took to find her mom's cookie recipe.

This time, it was a scratching at the window that made her scream.

Not loudly, but enough to make her feel embarrassed. Birds. Just birds. Or that raccoon that liked to ferret around their garbage cans at night. Determined to quit acting like a basket case, Gina resolutely ripped open a new bag of flour and started mixing the dry ingredients. Once she'd finished measuring and stirring those, she started adding the other ingredients, beginning with the eggs. She tapped the first egg on the side of the ceramic mixing bowl, breaking the shell neatly in half so the contents slid right out to sit on top of the brown pile of cocoa, sugar and flour. She did the same with a second egg, then a third and a fourth.

The phone rang, and she jumped, the reflexive motion of her hand sending the shell she'd been holding into the air. It landed on the counter with a gooey splat, and she frowned at it just before picking up the phone. "Hello?" she said.

"You only needed three," a voice she didn't recognize rasped.

"Excuse me?"

"Three eggs, not four."

Confused, Gina brought her hand to her cheek, belatedly realizing she'd probably left a smudge of cocoa on her face. "I don't—"

"Look at your recipe!"

The caller hung up, and the line went dead.

Gina punched the receiver button twice and listened. No dial tone.

The shadow in her house. The scraping at her window.

The awful feeling came slowly, held off by denial and disbelief. Half wondering if the call was just one of Max's stupid pranks, Gina jabbed at the receiver button again. Still no dial tone. Then she did what the caller had ordered and looked at the recipe.

Three eggs. Not four.

The dead phone fell out of her hands. "Oh, no," she sobbed, choking on her fear. She backed away from the counter, wondering where she could run, where she'd be safe. The shadow in her house. The scraping at her window.

Run behind her, and there was only her bedroom, with its flimsy door and tiny window. Run ahead, and she might make it outside, to the porch, where some neighbor might help.

She started forward, only to jerk back in horror as the doorknob turned on its own. Right. Then left. Right. Then left. She heard the small click when the lock gave, and then the door shot forward, only to be brutally halted in place by the door chain.

Whimpering now, Gina stepped backward, praying that the chain would hold, that someone would see. A heavy metal tool slipped between the door and the jamb, held by a bogeyman she'd never dreamed would actually come for her. The jaws opened, closed, and snapped the chain in two.

Nowhere to run.

Chapter Six

"Somehow, we have to convince the schools and universities to issue warnings, and maybe even the local papers. No woman should walk anywhere alone, especially after dark." Maggie tapped her black marker against the enormous white board she'd propped up against her office wall. She and Billy had worked well into the night on the eve of the killer's macabre October 8th anniversary. And now, after midnight, the results of their labor—a long list of notes about the Surgeon's signature characteristics—covered two-thirds of the board. Neither one of them were profilers, per se, but with Billy's near-photographic memory for things he'd read and her experience researching countless serial killers—not to mention her months of studying the Surgeon himself—they'd come pretty close. The FBI Behavioral Analysis Unit operated with less than 20 profilers and would have none to spare for a rogue agent and a crazy shut-in, but Billy and Maggie had done just fine on their own. She could feel it.

"We're going to need the police to handle that,"

Billy responded, scanning the list for the hundredth time. On the office floor next to where he sat lay a neat stack of manila folders, each filled with dozens of newspaper articles, computer printouts and photos.

"What about your people in San Francisco?" she asked, referring to Billy's FBI colleagues. "Is there anyone in the Violent Crimes Division who might assist? If we keep it quiet that you're involved?"

"The MPD has to invite the FBI in," he responded.

Uh-oh. Local versus federal law enforcement was a game she was all too familiar with. "Which they probably won't do until they see a second body in Monterey," she said.

"Which they won't do, period. I'm it, Maggie." A flash of irritation crossed his angular features.

Maggie lowered the marker and capped it with a click. "Dammit, Billy, why does this have to be so hard? He'll kill again. And if he wants to toy with me for a while, it'll be some innocent woman barely out of her teens." She pointed to the item on the list that read, Age range of victims: 18-32. "I don't know. Maybe I shouldn't have gone into hiding. Maybe if I were still in New Orleans, he would have stayed in his home territory, and we could have found him by now." Dropping the marker into a canister on top of her filing cabinet, she walked over to where Billy sat, lowering herself next to him. She reached over and straightened the already precisely stacked files between them.

He was staring at her. "What?" she asked.

"How did he find you?" he asked. His gray eyes

flicked to the board. "It's something we haven't talked about."

She pulled her knees toward her chest and toyed with the fringe on the hem of her worn jeans. "He always found me. I never knew how he did it."

"Always?" Billy prodded gently in that deep voice of his.

"He stalked me in New Orleans, after I...got away from him that time. He called, left notes. I'd go to the store, he'd tell me what I'd bought. I'd visit my family, he'd tell me what my mother was wearing." Her voice failed her for a moment, and she paused to get her bearings. "I had to leave. I was so afraid he'd hurt my family."

"So you came here?"

She nodded, focusing on the wooden strips dividing the window into small squares. "And as the months went by, I couldn't stop waiting for him to contact me again. I was always looking over my shoulder, always running. Eventually, it just got easier to stay inside."

"Until you couldn't go out."

"Yeah." She sighed. "I don't know how he does it." With that, she rose and started rearranging the objects on her immaculate desk.

Billy stood and walked over to the window seat, where he watched the ocean for a few moments. Maggie picked up yesterday's newspaper and was about to take it to the recycling bin in the kitchen when he broke the silence. "He started moving in this direction four months ago. What did you start doing differently around that time?"

She shrugged, almost laughed. "Not a whole lot. My sanity rests on a solid foundation of routine and boredom."

He turned to face her. "No, really. Think about it. Did your family talk to someone about you? Someone posing as an old friend, or your college alumni association?"

Maggie shook her head. "No. I've already warned them not to fall for something like that. They know better."

He stepped toward her, his expression intense. "Four months ago, either our killer had an epiphany about your whereabouts, or you started feeling safer and established some new form of communication with the outside world. Internet, phone, smoke signals. What did you do?"

"The FBI helped me get a phone number and credit card in Mary Smythe's name. I call my family sometimes, but we never discuss where or who I am." She absentmindedly rolled the newspaper in her hands as she thought back in time. "And I've always done that."

"Anything else?"

"I don't write letters. Ditto with the smoke signals." She batted the flat of one hand with the newspaper. "I don't know." Her eyes flicked to the bookcase behind her desk. "Oh, no."

"What?" He had moved to stand directly in front

of her, and his proximity was messing with her concentration. She took a step back.

"I ordered a book online. Using my own credit card." She pointed in the general direction of the shelf. "*Through the Looking Glass.* It was a favorite of mine as a kid, and I felt like reading it again."

"Bots."

"Bo—" Maggie moved her mouth around the unfamiliar word. "What? You know, the whole laconic man of mystery thing is charming, unless I really need to decipher what it is you're trying to say." She smiled at him, just so he'd know she was teasing him. Geez, no one could tell she was exhausted after a night of no sleep. "Do you think we might explore polysyllabic grunting today, Tarzan, or am I supposed to have a psychic understand of what 'bots' means?"

With patience that was really very charming, he explained in non-computer-geek language what bots were and how they could scour the Internet until they zeroed in on a target. "Credit card purchases make their job easier," he said. "If you build them right."

She fought the urge to cry. That day she'd braved buying a book over the Internet using her own name had seemed like such a triumph. But that was then. "Bots," she said. "It figures."

"They're how I found you."

The newspaper fluttered to the ground. "What?"

He winced. "I was desperate," he said.

She raised an eyebrow at him, already forgiving him, but wanting to make him squirm just a little. "You know, you're a little scary, Billy Corrigan."

He shoved his hands in his pockets, looking at her through a fringe of dark hair that had fallen into his eyes. "But you think the laconic man of mystery thing is charming, you said?"

Maggie laughed. "Oh, boy, do we need to sleep." Unbelievable that they were flirting with each other. She stifled a yawn with her fist, then turned and headed to the white board. Maybe not so unbelievable after so many hours without rest. "Our guy knows computers," she said. "Let's write that down, and then I need to crash." She looked over her shoulder at Billy as she grabbed her marker and scrawled something barely legible on the board. "You can sleep in one of the guest rooms, if you wan—"

At that moment, the scanner in the next room, which had been crackling and popping all evening, suddenly erupted in a flurry of sound. One word floated into the office, and that word sliced through her heart like a shard of ice.

Homicide.

Like a ghost, she dropped the marker and followed the sounds from the scanner, walking like a zombie into the kitchen. Billy moved in behind her.

The dispatcher's voice was firm and in control, but just a shade louder than any of her previous messages had been. "All units, assault, possible homicide at 1226 Forest Hills Road, twelve-twenty-six Forest Hills Road, at the intersection of Forest Hills and 121st Street. Three-Adam-One?"

Another voice crackled through the scanner.

"Three-Adam-One from Alvarado and East Franklin."

Slowly, Maggie raised her head and looked at him, the rest of her body temporarily frozen in place as the dispatcher continued to call MPD units to the homicide scene. She pressed her hands to her cheeks, rubbing them downward until they were clasped in a prayerlike fashion beneath her chin. She felt suddenly brittle, as if the slightest touch would cause her to crack into a million pieces. "It's him," she said.

"You don't know that," he said carefully.

But she did. She could feel it in her bones. You didn't study someone for almost two years and not develop some sort of bond with him, sick as it was.

Maggie moved closer to the scanner on the butcher table as the antique clock in the hallway behind them struck 4:00 a.m.

"All units responding to Forest Hills," the dispatcher said. "Reporting party arrived to find 33-year-old female possibly DOA. I had RP immediately leave the scene. More info when he calls back. All other units, code ten on channel one. Repeating code ten on channel one. Control clear, twenty-three-forty-one."

A helpless anger thrummed through her veins. She crossed her arms and tucked her hands under them, hoping that Billy hadn't seen them shaking. "She'll have dark, curly hair. It'll look like mine," she said, her voice dull and a monotone.

In a mere tenth of a second, Billy was there, right beside her, his presence somewhat comforting even as he was careful not to touch her. "Maggie, it's a big city. It could be anybody."

She wished she were the kind of person who collected useless knickknacks so she could break something. "No. It's him."

Through the haze of her emotions, she noticed his hands, clenched so tightly at his sides that the knuckles looked bloodless. There was a storm in his gray eyes and pure violence in the tightening of his jaw. It was almost as if the line between her rage and his had blurred until they were one and the same.

They stared at each other for a long moment, sharing the anger and an even deeper sense of helplessness. It was Maggie who came to her senses first. They needed to move. "Billy, can you…?" She stopped herself. She had no right to ask him that.

"Go to Forest Hills?" he asked, his voice so low and soft, she had to lean in to hear him. "Borkowski might let me in, especially if she's primary at the scene."

She nodded. "It would be great for someone to be my eyes and ears, since I can't—" She held out her hands, palms up, then let them drop to her sides in frustration. "Not that Borkowski will necessarily bend the rules for either one of us."

"If I go, who's going to stay with you?"

"I'll be fine." She paused, noticing how calm he looked, except for a barely there tightness in his jaw. Maybe she was being unfair. Maybe he'd have a chance to heal from his sister's death if he didn't immerse himself in crime scenes that were nearly identical. She'd been there when they'd found Jenna Corrigan. Though Billy had only seen photos, it was still no way to achieve closure after losing your last living family member. "It's you I'm worried about," she said, weighing her words. "You don't have to do this, Billy."

"I'm there," he cut her off abruptly. "But only if someone else can stay with you. Maybe Borkowski can get a uniform over here...."

"He won't come for me tonight." She started picking at a hangnail on her thumb. "He'll want to drag this out, taunt me somehow."

"Doesn't matter," Billy said.

It took only a few seconds for her to pick her skin until it bled. God, she wanted to keep him away from Forest Hills Road. She pressed her lips into a thin line, thinking. "How far back do you and Borkowski go as friends? Could you get a copy of the records? Crime scene photos? Lab results? Think you could charm the crime scene techs into sharing any theories about the choicest pieces of evidence?"

He shook his head. "That's not as good as being there, is it?"

"Of course it is," she lied. "Better in some ways."

He didn't quite smile at her, but something came alive in his gray eyes for the briefest moment. "You know, you suck at lying."

She grimaced and nodded. "When I was a cop, I had to sit in the background and seethe inwardly during interviews. I was a great bad cop." The joke felt hollow, but she turned her lips upward into some semblance of a smile anyway. Detach. She had to. One of them had to, so they could help the other one cross that line. Detachment meant sanity. Detachment was your only prayer of solving the case. Get your emotions entangled, and you'd make mistakes.

"I don't doubt it." With what she knew had to be forced casualness, he tossed her the cordless receiver from the phone table and fished his cell phone out of his pocket. The other pocket held one of those hands-free earpieces people liked to use while driving. He stuck it in his right ear, then plugged the other end of the long wire into his phone. "I'll call you as soon as I step out that door, and I won't stop talking to you until I walk back through it. If you hear anything suspicious, tell me, and I'll be back here in five minutes. In the meantime, I'm going to get on the radio and get someone over here pronto."

He'd followed her cue and was all business now. That was good. He'd need that composure when he saw the victim. Oh, would he need it.

Once at the door, Billy turned, a deep line forming between his eyebrows as the fingers of his right hand drummed an erratic beat on the doorframe. It wasn't difficult to read his mind.

"I'll tell you if I see or hear anything suspicious, I promise," she said.

"Good." He nodded, then stepped into the dark night.

Maggie swallowed hard. Obviously she hadn't detached enough, because it made her ill to send him off to that crime scene, where a brutal killer could very well be lurking in the shadows, watching the police. Watching Billy.

She nearly ran to the doorway, hitting the door with the flat palm of her hand to keep it from swinging shut. She gripped the edge of the doorframe and swung her upper body outward into the night.

"Be careful," she called after him as the security lamp attached to the garage automatically flicked on, flooding the front yard with a brilliant light. Billy halted at the sound of her voice, his body crouched half-in, half-out of his car door. He stared at her for a moment, nodded his head, then got all the way into the Crown Victoria and drove off.

It was only when she saw his taillights disappear from view that Maggie realized she'd been standing two steps outside her open doorway all this time.

"WHAT DO YOU SEE?"

Billy tapped the earpiece attached to his cell phone with one finger, lodging it further inside the inner curve of his ear. "Not a damn thing," he growled. "Crime scene techs won't let anyone in until they're finished bagging and tagging."

"Typical," Maggie responded. "And probably wise, but still annoying for us impatient types."

He noticed she was keeping her voice low and well-modulated, with the occasional smartass comment tossed at him to keep him on his toes. He wondered if she was doing the thing with her voice on purpose, to convey a subtle message. Stay calm. Stay cool. Don't lose your head, Billy.

"So we have a white, single-story house, with four stairs leading up to the front door. The back door is painted over, presumably sealed shut, and there are windows on all sides," Maggie said, echoing the first words he'd said to her upon arrival. "Since the techs are done outside, walk carefully around the house. What else do you see?"

Billy scanned the area in front of the bungalow, taking in the dozen squad cars that lined the narrow street, parked at haphazard angles indicating that their drivers had rushed to get out of the cars and into action. Blue and red lights circled around and around, casting an eerie, flickering glow on the uniformed officers and plainclothes detectives swarming about the area. A small crowd had formed outside the police perimeter, growing ever larger as people sleepily exited their homes to see what all the commotion was about. Down at the far end of the street, Billy could see the white Channel 7 news van, its drivers arguing heatedly with the cop who had halted their progress.

He walked around the small, bungalow-style house, staying as far from the white-painted exterior as he could so as not to disturb any evidence lying on the ground. Thankfully, this particular house had a little green around it, instead of being crammed up against its neighbors like many of the homes in Monterey, where real estate was at a premium. He took in the old, heavy glass windows; the imported grass, moist with dew; the sealed back door. The intact front door.

"No signs of forced entry," he said to Maggie as he circled around to the front of the house. "There's a depression in the bushes near one of the east-side windows, like he might have stood there and watched the victim, but he didn't use it as an entry point.''

"Hmmm."

"Social engineering?" he supplied.

"What?"

"Hacker term. Means you manipulated something to your benefit through personal contact. Charming people, as you put it."

"Oh." Maggie chewed on the thought for a moment. "That's not really his style. He takes the women by surprise. A rag dipped in chloroform, rohypnol—the 'date rape drug'—in a drink. If those don't work, he'll ambush you from behind and deliver a blow to the back of your head. If you're small enough, he'll come at you fast."

Billy watched the two crime techs from the state come down the rickety wooden stairs. Brentwood and Borkowski would be entering the house soon, and they'd be his ticket in. "So you don't think he'd change that?"

"No way. You can change locations, you can change basic M.O.s, but you'll never, ever change your signature if you're a serial killer. It's the mark of your personality, part of who you are, so it's the one part of the crime you can't control. The Surgeon probably isn't the most gregarious guy in the world. He's most likely a social misfit, so approaching a woman and trying to talk her into going somewhere quiet and secluded with him won't work. The only way to convince her when you're socially inept is to incapacitate her as fast as you can.''

"You keep saying 'you.' Is your opinion of me that low?'' he cracked, noticing Borkowski and Brentwood heading inside. Showtime.

"Get in his head, Billy. It's the only way to catch him.''

"Ni-i-ice,'' he drawled, his tone belying the fact that her words made his gut twist. Get inside the monster who'd murdered his sister. He'd rather get inside a boxing ring with the bastard. Bare-handed single combat. Let the best monster win.

"You okay, Billy?'' This time, instead of displaying that detached modulated tone she'd adopted, Maggie's voice was intimate, laced with concern. A voice that wrapped around his body and seeped into his bones. A voice that made him want...something.

"I'm fine.'' He shook it off and started up the steps.

A uniform who had followed the detectives inside the house came charging out the door and down the stairs. He nearly slammed into Billy while making his way to the patch of grass and flowering bushes below. In two seconds, the man was on his hands and knees, heaving up whatever had been in his stomach at five in the morning.

"What's going on? Billy, talk to me,'' Maggie said. Dammit, he wished she'd cut it out and go back to being impersonal.

He took his eyes off the cop and glanced up at the house. Borkowski stood in the doorway, and she waved him in with a sweep of her hand. If he hadn't known her for so long, he could have sworn she looked a little gray herself. Following Borkowski's lead, he stepped toward the door.

Borkowski gripped his elbow. He turned a questioning look at her.

"Brentwood had New Orleans fax in some notes from the Surgeon," she said, diving right into the important details. "We compared them to Maggie Reyes's note."

Billy drew in a deep breath. "And?"

"They match."

"So it really is the Surgeon?"

"Looks like," she said grimly. "Look, are you sure you need to go in there? I cleared you to move through it, but maybe you shouldn't..." Her words trailed off.

He just stared at her. "I'm in," he said into the mouthpiece dangling near his chin. Borkowski released his elbow, and he stepped past her into the house.

"Look, Billy," Maggie said into his ear, "you're just an observer. Go in and let me know exactly what you see, down to the last detail, and don't ever, *ever* let yourself feel anything. Whatever you do in Computer Crimes to distance yourself from the victim, do it now a thousand times over. Do it, or you'll go mad."

Too late, his mind screamed, but his body continued to climb the stairs. Distance. He could do this. Just a dispassionate observer.

He reached out to open the door, but the mere touch of his fingertips sent it swinging backward on creaking hinges. He glanced down at the handle. ''There are scratches on the door,'' he said, ''around the lockplate.''

''Tell me about the scratches,'' Maggie said, her tone once more still and calm and something he could center himself on.

''Small gouges, like he was using a tool, and it slipped. He must've picked the lock.''

''Smart guy,'' Maggie replied.

Billy leaned down to examine the scratches more closely. ''Not a lot of finesse, but it got the job done.''

''She didn't have any security locks?''

Billy walked around the open door and tapped it closed behind him with his foot. ''She had a security chain. He cut it in two.''

He heard Maggie's sharp intake of breath and knew exactly what she was thinking. It was the little details like that one that brought the crime into too-sharp focus, where you could almost imagine yourself in the victim's shoes, watching death as it snapped your locks and came for you.

''There's a bowl on the counter,'' he said abruptly. ''Blue, with dough inside. Looks like she was baking something.''

''Anything else?''

''Flour on the counter, spoon on the floor, cordless phone receiver next to it. There's a trail of flour heading into the living room, which is behind me and to the right. She heard him coming and backed or ran away. Probably picked up the phone to call for help. We should get the phone records. See if she reached anyone.''

''Tell me about the living room.''

Bracing himself, Billy stepped around the corner. He looked at the crumpled body lying in a puddle of blood on the room's cheap sisal rug. She was naked, except for the blue shirt that had been sliced down the center and hung off her bare shoulders. A section of the shirt near her collar was torn out, as if someone had ripped the material with his bare hands. Her arms and legs were flung out to the sides, and her wrist, which was so small, he could have wrapped his fingers around it twice, was marred by angry, red ligature marks. Scraps of fishing line were still wrapped around one wrist and both of her ankles. She'd been tied to something while he.... Billy found himself turning away from the girl and closing his eyes like a goddamned rookie.

It took some time before he found his voice again. ''You tell me,'' he said finally. ''Read it off our list.'' Probably a perverse request, but he knew that if Maggie could describe the scene before him, could pinpoint the Surgeon's ''calling cards,'' as she'd put it, without looking, they would both know for certain exactly what they were dealing with.

Silence. Just when he thought he'd gone too far, she started to speak. ''She's a young woman, probably in her 20s or early 30s. She'll have multiple ligature marks on her neck. He likes to strangle his victims to the point of unconsciousness and then revive them. Again and again and again.''

She paused to let that piece of information sink in. He'd rather she hadn't. ''Why?''

Stupid question, but she answered it anyway, her voice flat. ''Makes him feel powerful. He holds the power of life and death over the victim. It's an effective way to terrorize someone.''

She ought to know.

Maggie went on. ''Since he attacked her head-on, my guess is he came at her running and delivered a blow to the head with a large, blunt object, like a baseball bat or a hammer. The head wound shouldn't be hard to spot.''

It wasn't. ''Baseball bat,'' he supplied. ''Or something large and rounded, with no sharp corners. There's medium blood spatter on the wall close to the dining room/kitchen entrance.''

''His main hobby is picquerism—meaning she'll have multiple cuts all over her body, both pre-and post-mortem—and there will be signs of bondage with fishing line. In the past, he's liked to sketch a very precise grid on the victim's lower abdomen. Five lines vertical, three horizontal. Any large stab wounds—the ones that gave him his name—will be inside those lines, made with a hunting knife with a serrated top edge.''

He reminded himself to detach, to forget that the woman covered in blood and other substances had once been beautiful, vibrant, *alive*.

Like his sister.

"Stay with me, Billy," Maggie's voice said in his ear. "I need you."

"I'm here," he responded, taking his eyes off the victim to focus on the walls. The blood-spattered walls. "You're right." She knew so much about this killer, too much, and that knowledge had put a question inside his head about a night in New Orleans eighteen months ago. It was a question he didn't dare ask. Not here. "About all of it."

"Does she have black hair?" Maggie asked, her strong voice suddenly sounding smaller, more afraid. "Curly, like mine?"

Billy shoved his hands through his own hair, which caught and pulled on the latex gloves he'd forgotten he was wearing. "Yes."

Something about the victim's shirt still nagged at him. "Maggie, does he take trophies?"

"What, the Surgeon?" Maggie responded, caught off-guard. "Yes. Not all of the families of his past victims could tell whether something was missing, but there were six who said he'd taken things. One ring, two necklaces, various pieces of clothing and an ear-ring. Why?"

"Jenna was missing her locket when we found her," he said. The thought of that monster keeping the heart-shaped locket his sister had treasured made him want to smash something.

"I know, Billy. I'm sorry."

Detach. He had to detach. He told her about the shirt.

"Anything else I missed?" Maggie's voice broke

the silence again. He clenched his teeth until his jaw ached and concentrated on the task at hand.

"Defense wounds," he said.

"What?"

"Broken fingernails, scratches on her arms, bruises on her face." He paused, inhaling deeply through his mouth. "She fought back."

Maggie was silent. Billy looked away and waited for her to get past the emotion that was nearly choking him. "Good for her," she whispered. So much for detachment.

How he managed to stay, he'd never know. But stay he did, reporting all the minute details of the house and the crime scene to Maggie. That done, he wove around the detectives who were milling through the rooms in respectful silence and finally headed for the front door.

As he was about to leave, his eye caught something bright that he hadn't noticed earlier. He walked over to the small microwave oven. A birthday card.

After reporting its existence to Maggie, he carefully flipped it open with one latex-covered finger.

"Happy birthday to the best roomie ever. Love, Gina," Billy read aloud.

His eyes went to the trail of flour on the floor. *Don't have a name. Not now.*

"She has a roommate," Maggie said, sadly.

"The second bedroom I saw in the back," Billy concurred. "I'll ask Borkowski and Brentwood if anyone's contacted her friends and family." He pushed open the door and stepped outside.

Almost immediately, he noticed a yellow Volkswagen Beetle parked haphazardly just outside the police perimeter, as if the driver had come to a sudden stop. A young blond woman next to the car gestured emphatically as she talked to the officer Billy had seen in the bushes earlier. He took the stairs at a fast walk, almost a run.

Out of the corner of his eye, he saw Borkowski move to rescue the cop, who tugged at the collar of his blue uniform shirt, obviously out of his element. He reached the small group just as the young woman stepped around the cop, unconsciously reaching for Elizabeth. "Please," she begged, her eyes flicking from Elizabeth to Billy. "Has something happened to Gina?"

Gina, Jenna. They sounded the same. *We regret to inform you that there's been an incident involving your sister.*

"What's your name, miss?" Borkowski asked gently.

The woman's eyes widened, and she latched on to the question with a gratitude that nearly undid Billy.

"Kelli. Kelli Ransom." She wrapped her arms around her thin frame. "Gina is my roommate."

Was. Gina was. Not is. Billy felt hysterical laughter bubbling up in his chest, and he fought to choke it back down. *Don't lose your head, Corrigan.*

Borkowski scrawled something in the small notebook she'd brought to the scene, the corners of her wide mouth tipped downward in a frown. "Were you with her at all today?"

"No." Kelli shook her head. "I was in Vegas this weekend, visiting my parents. Where's Gina? Can I see her?"

"I'm sorry, Ms. Ransom." Though Borkowski's voice was gentle, she kept her face schooled in an impassive, faintly sympathetic expression. Detached. Billy couldn't help but wish he could cultivate the same expression, and the feeling behind it.

Jenna Rose Corrigan was found dead at 0610 in an abandoned building at 1612 Chartres Ave. He fought the urge to turn and walk away as fast as he could.

Borkowski put her notepad down. "Your room-mate—"

"It's my birthday," Kelli interrupted almost frantically, tugging on the zipper of her green sweater. Her eyes darted around the scene, from the yellow tape across her front door to the state van the crime scene techs had come in. "Gina's planning a party. We're having a party tomorrow night."

The cause of death was an apparent homicide. The assailant remains at large. No further information is available at this time.

"Elizabeth—" Billy forced himself to murmur.

Detective Borkowski twirled her pen between her fingers, a nervous habit he recognized, and tried again. "Ms. Ransom, we deeply regret to inform you—"

"Elizabeth, stop," Billy broke in. She might have to detach to keep her head night after night on this job, but he couldn't, he wouldn't listen to that damned canned speech. No one should have to find out they'd lost their best friend. Not that way.

The detective's head swiveled in his direction. "What are you—?"

The look he shot her was enough to make Bor- kowski back away. "I'll tell her," he said.

Kelli clamped a shaking hand over her mouth. "No." She backed away until her body smacked against the side of her car, her voice breaking on that small, insignificant word.

Borkowski nodded, and Billy moved in between them. Kelli clutched her stomach and bent at the waist, moaning softly as her other hand scrabbled for a hold on Billy's arm.

Billy put his hand under Kelli's elbow, supporting her until she fell forward into his arms. Then he told her, without mincing words, what had happened to her best friend. She cried for hours, while waiting for her parents to arrive from Vegas, and he held on to her the entire time.

Chapter Seven

The first brilliant rays of dawn were bleeding into the sky when Maggie heard Billy pull into her driveway. He'd promised to stay on the phone with her until he returned, and that he'd done. But he hadn't said a word to her since he'd left the crime scene. She'd heard bits and pieces of conversation he'd had with a woman who had probably been the victim's roommate, but it wasn't enough to know what he'd just been through. She wondered whether the aftermath of the crime scene had been even worse than seeing Gina Markson's crumpled, brutalized corpse.

She heard him get out of the car and slam the door shut, the bang reverberating up the driveway to where she stood at the window. Looking pale and exhausted, he marched up the sand and gravel to her front door. The loud, banging knock told her all she needed to know about his current state of mind.

She let him in, and he stalked past her as she closed the door. When he finally turned to face her, she noticed he wasn't looking at her, but at something just to the left of her that only he could see.

"He tortured her," he said in a flat, emotionless voice. "It must have taken hours."

"I know." Maggie leaned back against the door, her hands behind her back gripping the brass door-knob. She wished to heaven she could tell him the young woman hadn't known what it was that had killed her. But that would be a lie.

"Her boyfriend found her early this morning, after coming back from a road trip with his buddies." Billy laughed, an eerie sound completely devoid of humor. "Another poor jerk who'll spend the rest of his life wondering why he wasn't there when she needed him."

Maggie pushed off from the door and walked to stand directly in front of him. "That's not true, Billy."

He closed his eyes and winced, turning his face away from her as if to hide the dark, restless grief inside him. His breath was harsh and gasping as he spun around and headed into the kitchen. Without stopping to consider if it was the best option, Maggie followed.

As soon as he reached the far wall, with its window overlooking the sea, he halted, raising his hands slowly above his head in a gesture that looked re-markably like surrender. The steady movement couldn't hide the tension in his back, his muscles, his shaking hands.

"Please, Billy," Maggie said, but she didn't know what she was asking.

His hands moved behind his head and gripped the

back of his neck, and for a split second, it looked like he was going to pull himself together. But then his left hand clenched into a fist and shot out like a piston, punching the wall with a sudden, vicious force that startled her. Once. Twice. Three times.

The blows stopped as suddenly as they'd begun. Billy turned, revealing bleeding knuckles, and opened his mouth to speak. Then, he just shook his head, probably knowing full well there were no words that could encompass what he'd seen earlier that day. Maggie reached for him, and he stumbled forward and wrapped his arms around her.

His body shook so hard she thought he'd lift her off the ground. She stroked his hair, his back, whispered meaningless words of comfort into his ear. He ran his hands up her arms to her shoulders, finally clenching his fists around the material of her shirt. "God, her face," he ground out.

"I'm sorry, Billy," Maggie said, holding him as tightly as she could. "I'm so sorry."

He pushed her gently away and reached behind him, gripping the back of one of the kitchen chairs for support. "I should've been there," he gasped, running a hand across his face. "Why wasn't I there?"

"There's no way you could—" She halted her sentence as understanding dawned. How could she be so dense? He wasn't talking about Gina Markson at all.

Maggie reached up and took his face in her hands, tipping his head toward her so he would focus on her words. "Billy, listen to me. It didn't happen that way with Jenna. I promise you, she wasn't—" Maggie paused, choosing her next phrase carefully. ''He didn't spend that much time with her. I doubt if she felt much at all.''

Billy shook his head, dislodging her hands as he backed away, looking at her as if she were a life raft and he a drowning man. ''You can't know that.''

''I do,'' she said firmly.

''How?''

''I don't think—''

Once again, Billy gripped the back of his neck with both hands, a storm in his gray eyes. ''Tell me how you know, Maggie, and don't lie to me. Not about this.''

Detachment. After so many years of being a cop, then being a crime writer who investigated the most gruesome homicides imaginable, detachment should have been easy for her. But instead, she found herself wanting desperately to bring even a moment's peace into Billy's life. Once again, instinct took over before she could think through her actions. She reached down to take one of his hands in hers and slipped it under the hem of her button-down shirt, where he could touch the scars on her stomach. ''He escalated with me.''

Billy blinked, startled for just a moment out of the black emotion that ruled him. They remained utterly still for a moment, then his fingers started fluttering against the raised, white tissue on her abdomen. He bent his head, gently tugging the hem of her shirt upward with his free hand.

Reflexively, she tightened her grip on the hand she

held, pushing his other away with her elbow. Touching was one thing. Seeing was another thing entirely.

"Everything before me was experimentation. I was the first—" She swallowed. Why was this so difficult? Detach, dammit. "The first one he took his time with before the kill. Before me, he dealt quickly with his victims and inflicted the wounds postmortem."

She closed her eyes and leaned forward. He must've bent his head, because she was able to touch her forehead to his, as if to borrow some of his strength so she could keep standing. "I'm so sorry you lost your sister. But I can tell you this, and it's the honest truth—as the fourth victim, she didn't know what was happening to her. She didn't feel a thing."

He pulled her into his arms once more and held her so tightly, she almost couldn't feel that he was shaking. They stood like that for several minutes, and she was so aware of his hands around her waist, his breath on her cheek. She couldn't help but feel that in another life, at another time, they might have been friends. Or even something more.

Just before he pulled away, she felt him brush his mouth against her forehead. "Thank you," he whispered into her hair.

How ridiculous, that he should thank her for such a grim revelation. "I wish I could have saved her for you," she said, studying her hands after he'd retreated, not trusting herself to look at him right away. "I wish she were here and neither of you had ever heard of the Surgeon."

"I know, Mags," he said, the new nickname providing the sense that they were in their own world, horrible as it was.

"We'll find him. I promise," she said, but it sounded hollow as she thought about how it would still be too late for Jenna, Tess, Carrie, Janine, and all the other victims, now including young, innocent Gina Markson.

"I'll have someone stand watch at the door," he said. "I have to get out of here for awhile," he said.

"I know. It gets too ugly in here sometimes."

He shook his head, the corner of his mouth turning up in a sad half smile. He touched her cheek then, and she couldn't help but be startled by the gesture. "No, it's beautiful in here."

Then he took his hand away and headed outside. Maggie watched him through the window as he walked down the sand, until she couldn't see him anymore, then turned and headed into her office. She had work to do.

WHEN BILLY RETURNED to her house, he was wearing a sweat-drenched T-shirt and a pair of navy sweatpants. His hair was plastered to his forehead, and his tennis shoes were full of sand. Obviously he'd been for a run on the beach. A four-hour run. She let him in and was surprised when James Brentwood and Elizabeth Borkowski pushed through behind him.

"We'd like to talk to you, Ms. Reyes," Detective Borkowski said, in what Maggie was fast recognizing as her typical no-nonsense manner.

"Sure. But it's Maggie, not Ms. Reyes." She led them into the living room, and when they were all seated with cans of diet soda and tumblers of ice in front of them—given out in a futile pretense that they were all having a normal visit in the middle of their normal lives—the two detectives got right down to business.

"Maggie, what happened to Gina Markson last night is strikingly similar to Abby Rhodes's murder," Brentwood said, pouring his soda into the glass. To any outside observer, they might look as if they were having a tea party. "Agent Corrigan has informed us about your track record working on these kinds of cases."

"We've got a serial killer on our hands," Borkowski broke in bluntly. She explained the handwriting analysis they'd had performed on the Surgeon's notes from New Orleans and the one Maggie had recently discovered on her door. "We're pretty certain now that the Surgeon is in our city, and he's murdered two young women on our watch. We need your help." The can of soda Maggie had given her sat on the coffee table, unopened.

"We're forming an ad hoc task force to work on the Markson and Rhodes cases," Brentwood said. "We'd like you on it."

Maggie blinked in surprise. Now that, she hadn't been expecting. "You know I'll help you any way I can, but I've been out of the game for awhile. I'm not sure what I can do." Remembering Billy's hint about the MPD's problems with federal law enforcement, she asked, "Why not just call in the FBI?" As far as she was concerned, the more resources the Monterey Police had, the better.

Brentwood leaned forward, resting his elbows on his knees. His fingers tapped restlessly against the soda glass. "Chief Dominic has, uh, issues with calling in the feds."

Borkowski moved closer to the edge of the oversized chair, her calves sandwiched between it and the matching ottoman. "The feebies working with us back in August on the last high-profile homicide we had were so wedded to their profiles, they refused to admit that our guy had deviated. Had us looking for an impoverished Latino when the perp was an upperclass Caucasian man. That little episode had the NAACP in our faces for a long time. Dominic would rather work with a freelance expert like you than one of them any day." She cocked her head at Billy. "No offense."

Billy shrugged in response. He was the only member of their party who hadn't sat down, preferring instead to stand near the window. "None taken," he said in his deep voice.

Maggie took a swallow of her diet soda and set the glass on the table with a thunk. "Translation: Chief Dominic likes my experience, but he likes the fact that I'm not likely to storm into the station and try to take over the case even more, right?"

Maggie's comment had Brentwood fiddling with his tie, but Borkowski just smirked. "Would you be insulted if I told you you'd pegged the chief to a T?"

"Nah." Maggie shrugged. "I'm not crazy about the 'us versus them' attitude between the FBI and some local cop shops, but it never surprises me when you all start playing King of the Mountain."

Borkowski reached into the battered briefcase that rested on top of the ottoman and pulled out a stack of manila envelopes and file folders. She tossed them on the glass-and-ironwork coffee table. "This is everything we got on Gina Markson, as well as the info our friends in Little Rock and Denver were willing to share. St. Louis is being a little more stubborn about procedure, but we should get their files soon."

"We heard you're our best shot at predicting this guy's next move," Brentwood interjected, shooting a quick glance in Billy's direction. "If Gina Markson really was killed by the Surgeon, we're going to need that kind of advantage."

"I wish I had a crystal ball, James," Maggie responded. "But I'll do what I can."

"There's something else you need to see." Borkowski pulled a plastic evidence bag out of her briefcase and laid it on the table in front of Maggie. Inside was a note, with handwriting that appeared identical to the note that had been impaled on her door earlier that week.

"She looks like you...should," Maggie read. She thought about the photo he'd sent her, of the woman with the black curly hair that looked so much like her own. "Were there any photographs this time?"

Brentwood shook his head. "It's too early to tell

if he means you, but we thought it was best to keep you in the loop.''

Maggie turned the note over and handed it back to the detectives. And she tried not to think too hard about poor Gina Markson.

''In the meantime, we're going to start asking staff at local hotels if they've seen anything suspicious. He's not local, and we figure he needs a place to stay,'' Brentwood said.

Maggie nodded her approval. ''Good plan. You might want to talk to people at local real estate offices. He may have rented a place of his own, so he has some privacy.''

Borkowski nodded. ''With your permission, Agent Corrigan here has agreed to move into your spare bedroom as part of our twenty-four/seven protection plan for you.'' She reached up to brush her short, curly hair out of her eyes. ''We'll step up those extra patrols we've been sending to your neighborhood. If anything else happens, I think we can talk the chief into putting a couple of officers outside your door.''

Maggie blinked. Billy Corrigan in her house, in her space, twenty-four/seven. Wow. ''I didn't realize you'd even started sending cars past my house,'' she said, taking pains to keep her voice neutral.

Brentwood looked mildly offended at her statement. ''I gave you my word, Maggie.''

''Of course,'' she said, putting as much apology in her voice as she could manage. ''But Billy?'' She looked over to where he stood, leaning near the window facing the trees outside her house. ''Are you sure moving in is necessary?'' Part of her loved the thought of having him around, and another part of her wanted to throw him out bodily and keep him away. At least until she was able to go outside and meet him.

''You said he's focusing on you as his key to immortality,'' Billy said. ''I want to make sure you survive it.''

''I should probably protest, but I'm glad to have you here,'' she said simply.

He nodded, then pulled his car keys out of his back pocket. ''I'm heading back to San Francisco to pick up some things. Be back in a few hours.''

Brentwood rose, and Borkowski followed suit. ''We'll be right outside until he gets back,'' Brentwood said as he shoved his arms into the tan overcoat.

''Thank you,'' she said, wondering if she'd be able to do enough for them to merit this kind of care. She only hoped that she could.

THE NEXT COUPLE of days were quiet, which was to be expected. The Surgeon would most likely lay low for a few days, choosing his next victim, watching her, waiting until the murderous impulse grew too strong once more to ignore. And in the meantime, Maggie was stumbling through the dark, trying to find some clue that would bring him into focus so he would no longer be a nameless, faceless killer.

Maggie put down the report she'd been holding and rubbed her temples. Another sleepless night, and she had nothing to show for it. Her body ached, she was so tired, but she couldn't sleep. She wouldn't.

Billy reached across the desk and slid the file she'd dropped toward him. He'd worked by her side the entire time, poring over each file as she finished with it. It had turned into such a comfortable routine, it didn't register at first what he was about to look at. But then it did register, and she felt sick thinking about what was going to happen when he saw the picture at the top of that file.

"Don't—" She swiped at the folder, but her fingers only closed on air.

Two seconds later, he'd thrown Jenna Corrigan's folder back on her desk, his expression shuttered. All except those too-expressive eyes. "Billy?" she said. *Talk to me.*

In the background, she heard the faint sound of tires crunching on sand and gravel. "Someone's here," he said, and then he left the room. A few seconds later, she heard him exchange a few words with Adriana, and then the door slammed. No doubt he was already on the other side of it, on his way out for another punishing run.

Maggie scooped the papers that had fallen out of Jenna Corrigan's file back inside the folder and added it to the neat stack beside her. She should be used to this by now. For the past few days, he'd kept his conversations with her professional, his expression guarded and remote, almost as if he were feeling awkward about letting her into the darkness of his emotions after finding Gina Markson. Anytime their dialogues took a personal turn, he'd clam up entirely. On a couple of occasions, she thought she heard him whisper his sister's name.

Though she ached to know the magic words that would make him whole again, Maggie knew there was nothing she could say or do that would help. And maybe it was better that they focus on the work, instead of forging a personal connection. After all, the last thing anyone needed was to befriend an agoraphobic.

Turning her mind to the task in front of her, Maggie sifted through the photos and files Brentwood and Borkowski had given her. Then the small digital clock stuck to her computer monitor beeped, distracting her once more. Every second that ticked by was one second closer to one more young woman's death—and she wasn't any closer to finding the Surgeon. Judging by her brief contacts with Borkowski, Brentwood and the small task force they were in the process of assembling, the police hadn't discovered anything new, either. The Surgeon would kill again, and the chance that they'd be able to stop him in time grew slimmer with each passing moment.

Adriana walked into the office, trailing small feathers from the marabou trim on her black, knee-length cardigan, holding an organic root beer in each hand. She set one can on the desk in front of Maggie and popped the top on the other. Obviously, she wasn't about to give up her habit of checking up on Maggie after her Saturday yoga class, even though she knew Billy was staying at the house.

"*Chica,* you're shedding." Maggie pressed her finger down onto a piece of fluff that had floated near her, pinning it to the desktop. After three tries, it successfully adhered to her skin, so she rubbed her forefinger and thumb rapidly together over the wastebasket until it rolled off and floated inside.

"You like it?" Addy performed a slow twirl to give Maggie the full view of the sweater, causing more feather bits to fly free into the air like tiny paratroopers. "Someone brought it into the Diva the other day, and I couldn't bear to give it away."

"Yeah, can't have you making money or anything," Maggie said with a laugh.

"Hey," Adriana swept one hand down her sweater front. "I'm a walking billboard for my store. It is my duty to look funky yet fashionable at all times." She threw herself into one of the small padded chairs in front of Maggie's desk and put her feet up on one corner of the desk. "So, tell me about the computer geek."

Maggie made a noise that was half snort, half laugh. "I never said he was a geek."

Adriana took a sip of her root beer. "You never told me he was a *papi chulo,* either."

"He's not that pretty," Maggie said, shuffling some papers in an attempt to look casual. Okay, he *was* that pretty, if a scruffy, testosterone-laden renegade agent like Billy could be described that way, but she wasn't about to admit it.

Adriana narrowed her eyes. "Ah, so that's how it is."

"What? That's how what is?"

"Never mind," Adriana singsonged. "You'll tell me when you're ready. Tell me what you're working on." Dropping her feet to the floor, Adriana leaned forward and idly flipped open one of the folders on Maggie's stack. "Ick." She then promptly closed it again.

"Yeah, don't open those," Maggie said. "This stuff does nothing for your chi."

Twisting a lock of her caramel-brown hair, which today was streak-free, Adriana finished her soda in silence, the look on her face morphing from playful to worried. "Do you really think getting involved with cases like these again is such a good idea?" She put the can down on the desk and ambled with easy grace to the window seat, tucking her tall frame into the cushioned space. She obviously preferred to look at the fog and the ocean rather than crime scene pictures.

Using her fingertips, Maggie pushed a few photos around her desktop as if they were a pile of playing cards, finally choosing one to pick up and examine more closely. "I don't think I have a choice, you know?" She squinted at the picture of Gina Markson and brought it closer to her face.

"Hmmm." Addy hugged her knees to her chest, her fingers toying with the flared hems of her trendy black yoga pants. While Adriana studied the ocean, Maggie stood and took her abandoned soda can into the kitchen, picking up feather bits along the way.

When she came back, Addy hadn't moved from her perch.

"You know," Adriana said without turning her head, "Master Rishi at the meditation center once said that if you want a beautiful life, you should surround yourself with beauty. That—" She waved a graceful hand toward the pictures and files. "—is *so* not beauty."

Maggie sat down on the floor, using the front of the desk to prop up her back. "What would you do in my place?"

Addy glanced at the fog swirling across the ocean and traced a finger down the piece of wood that bisected the window glass as she pondered her answer. "I don't know. Move to Bora Bora and become a florist, maybe." She pushed off the window seat and moved to sit down next to Maggie. "*Mira,* I've known you since college. I know what you've been through, and I know what scares you so much that you can't leave your house. But what I do not understand is why you won't just leave this to the authorities? *Por el amor de Dios,* why do you have to look at those pictures?" She sighed softly and examined her hands, her silver rings glinting in the sunlight. "Let them handle this, Maggie. Maybe we can get you back to New Orleans somehow. I can close the store and stay with you there until it's over."

Like Addy could afford to shut the Trashy Diva down for even a few days. The store did well, but, like most small businesses, the line between financial success and bankruptcy was a thin one, even with the twice-a-week yoga classes tacked on. "I appreciate that offer more than you know, but you've done so much for me already." Maggie placed both of her hands over one of Adriana's and squeezed, hoping the touch could somehow convey how grateful she was for their friendship and Addy's selflessness.

Addy squeezed back. "Friendships like this one are rare," she said. "I can say anything to you. Always could. And I know, I *know* you would do the same for me." She dropped Maggie's hand and twisted her body to look her square in the eye. "It's been a privilege. Really."

It took Maggie about two seconds of intense deep breathing before she lost it. "Oh, no, you're going to make me cry." She fanned herself with one hand while biting down hard on her lower lip. "Okay, okay, I'm not losing it, I'm not, I'm fine, I'm fine." They both laughed, and then the moment passed.

"I'm not asking you to keep checking up on me and doing things for me, because there's no point in hiding anymore," Maggie began. "It's just...I can't leave."

"Why not?" Adriana didn't look happy. She tugged at her voluminous sweater until she found the pocket and took out a piece of gum. In a flurry of movement, she unwrapped it and shoved the gray stick in her mouth. A few seconds later, she and the gum were making noises like a small firecracker.

Which was so unlike the normally elegant Adriana Torres. "What's with the gum lately? I thought you grew out of that after senior-year exams?"

"It's gross, I know." Without getting up, Addy reached an arm up and grabbed a tissue from the box on the edge of Maggie's desk. "Nervous habit, recently resurrected, because yoga just doesn't cut it when there's a serial killer after your best friend— don't tell my students." She deposited the gum in the tissue and tossed the whole wad in the trash. "You still haven't answered my question. Why won't you leave?"

Maggie blew out a breath. "I don't know. I'm sick of waiting for the other shoe to drop, I suppose."

"That's a big, scary shoe you're waiting for." Addy got up and paced across the room. She pulled off her cardigan with angry, jerky movements, revealing a peach baby T with the words Think Globally, Stretch Locally printed on the front. Using more force than necessary, she threw the sweater on top of the small filing cabinet to her left. "You make me so...*enojada* sometimes. He's going to *kill* you."

Mad. Adriana was getting mad. Maggie rubbed her eyes with the heels of her hands and sighed. Adriana tried hard to be the embodiment of inner peace and balance, but when she started throwing the word *enojada* around, things could get ugly. "Sometimes, I think catching this creep is the only thing that'll make me better."

"Maybe not putting yourself in the path of a murdering psychotic would make you more better, you know? *Ay,* I am through arguing with you, you stubborn *burra.*" Glowering at her one last time, Adriana dropped into a lotus position on the floor and placed her hands, palms up, on her knees. She touched the thumb and middle finger of each hand together, closed her eyes, and began taking deep breaths through her nose and blowing them out of her mouth.

"Addy, stop that."

"I am inner peace and balance," Addy muttered, her eyes still closed.

"Really, Addy, don't you think you're being a little bit of a drama queen here?"

"I am balance and harmony. I will not let the fact that you are acting like a suicidal mule throw my emotions out of alignment any more than they already are."

"A mule? Thanks a lot." Maggie said, though her thoughts were slowly drifting toward a conclusion she was sure Adriana was going to hate.

It didn't take long. After a few seconds of silence, Addy opened one eye. "You're quiet."

"You're going to hate this," Maggie said. "But I need you to leave me alone for a few months. I have to know you're safe."

Adriana let loose a string of rapid Spanish that would have made her mother's hair curl, inner balance and harmony apparently forgotten.

"It was one thing when the Surgeon was far away, but he's here, Addy," she pleaded. "He's watching my house. He's watching you. I want you safe."

"And I don't want you dead," Adriana countered. "No way. No freaking way am I going anywhere. Who would bring your groceries?" She threw her hands in the air, shaking the backs of her palms at

Maggie in a terrific impression of an Italian mother. "Who would bring you extra aspirin when you have a headache? Who would remind you to do your yoga? And this house!" She stood and picked up a chair Maggie had left in the center of the room, then carried it to the east wall. "You keep leaving things in places that interrupt the chi flow. Who's going to fix that? That Billy Corrigan? Ha."

The change in tone made Maggie sit up. "Ha? He's a federal agent."

"Ha-ha-ha. From what you've told me, he's more messed up than that two of us put together."

"Addy, I couldn't have better protection, which is more than I can say for you. Please, can't you just—"

Addy snorted. "That man is trouble."

"He's not."

"Just you wait. I have a bad feeling about that Agent Corrigan, and I always trust my feelings," she said, folding one hand over her lower ribcage, as if her intuition was centered in the core of her body. "Something awful is going to happen. I don't care how good-looking he is."

"Uh, I came at a bad time, didn't I?" a deep voice asked.

Maggie looked up to see Billy leaning against the doorframe, holding a glass of water in one hand and another set of files in the other. Since he wasn't drenched in sweat, she figured he hadn't been outside for a run. He turned to Maggie, tossing the files on the desk. "Coroner's report," he said.

A dark look on her pretty face, Adriana stalked

over to the filing cabinet and grabbed her sweater. Shoving her arms into the sleeves, she stalked past Billy and out the door.

A moment later, she returned with a carpet sweeper. "I hope you now realize how much our friendship means to me, Reyes," she snarled as she vacuumed pieces of black fluff off the carpet. "I spoiled a perfectly good exit just because I know how much you'd hate it if I didn't clean up after this stupid sweater."

When Maggie opened her mouth to reply, Adriana put a hand up to stop her words. "No, don't say anything. I want you to take a few hours to process what I said, and think about honoring yourself by doing what's healthy for you." She spun around and pushed the carpet sweeper toward the door, stopping directly in front of Billy. "I hope you know what you're doing, asking her to get involved with this case, because if anything happens to her, I will hunt you down." With that, she literally swept past him. A few seconds later, they heard Adriana let herself out the front door with a slam.

Billy leaned against a corner of the desk. "Your friend is kind of scary."

Maggie smiled, though part of her mind was still occupied by the ugliness she'd brought into her friend's life. Adriana had made too many sacrifices for her in the past year and a half, and the guilt of it weighed on Maggie every day. "She's just overprotective," she finally said. Without getting up, she scooted across the floor to lean her back against the wall. "She's been that way ever since we were in college together."

"That's where you met?"

Maggie nodded. "Freshman year roommates. She was majoring in physics, which is really weird when you think about the fact that she now owns a thrift store and teaches yoga." Maggie shrugged.

"Ah." With a casual grace, Billy ambled over to a small table she kept in the corner of the room. It was just large enough for the cheap chessboard that lay on top, the pieces arranged as if someone had left them there mid-game. "You two play?" he asked.

"We used to, but Addy now prefers to align my chi when she comes over." Maggie hugged her knees to her chest, picking at an imaginary piece of lint on the legs of her gray fitted sweatpants. "I play by myself sometimes. Helps me think."

He picked up a pawn and twirled it between his fingers. "Rusty?"

"You wish."

"How do you feel about utter humiliation?"

Somehow, he managed to ask the question with a straight face, and it was all she could do not to burst out laughing. Instead, she shot him an exaggerated sneer and rose to sit on the side of the table with the white pieces. "How do you feel about eating crow?"

He put the chess piece back on the table, then spun the chair around and straddled it. "Not today, Mags." He smiled at her, an expression that seemed slightly alien on his face since she'd never seen him really smile before. Maybe it was inappropriate for them to be joking around mere days after Gina Markson was discovered, but Maggie wasn't about to deny them the one moment of normalcy they'd shared since they'd met, no matter how illusory it might have been.

She started picking up the plastic pieces and arranging them into straight rows on either side of the board. "Didn't know you were the type to talk smack, Agent Corrigan. Especially when you're not going to be able to back it up."

Billy put the last bishop into its place on the board. "Just for that, I'll let you go first."

"You're too good to me." With two fingers, Maggie pushed one of her pawns forward two spaces. She watched Billy as he moved to respond. "Am I the only one who's finding it strange that we're having a normal conversation?"

He moved a pawn on the opposite end of the board forward one space and put his hands on the chair back, leaning his chin on them. "Enjoy it while you can," he said. "I'm in no hurry to start discussing those files on your desk anytime soon."

They concentrated on making their next few moves, then Maggie broke the silence. "So, what kind of music do you listen to?"

"I don't. Not anymore."

She blinked and sacrificed one of her pawns to his bishop. "Favorite food?"

His dark eyebrows drew together, but otherwise, his focus seemed wholly on the game before them. "You know, I don't remember. You?"

"My mother's homemade caramel flan, which I haven't had since—" She stopped, not wanting to think about the circumstances under which she'd left New Orleans. "Watch much TV?"

"Destroyed the TV set with a baseball bat. Right after the stereo."

"Ah." With a small flourish, she took one of his bishops with her castle.

"Are you seeing anyone?"

The question was so unexpected, she nearly dropped the bishop she was holding.

Billy looked up from the board, and one corner of his mouth turned up in a crooked smile. "I'm not hitting on you, Mags. Just wondering if there's a boyfriend who might not like my being here while he's away on business, or something."

Mags, again. She should probably nip that unsophisticated nickname in the proverbial bud, but it was growing on her. "No, no boyfriend. Dating's a little tough when the thought of leaving your house for dinner and a movie terrifies you." She put the chess piece on the table and smiled back at him. "How about you?"

"No, not since..." His voice trailed off, and then he ducked his head. "No." He took one of her remaining pawns with his queen.

They made their next few moves in silence, leaving Maggie feeling awkward over spoiling their fragile rapport. She tried again. "What do you do for fun, outside of work?"

He tapped a rhythm on one of his knights while

pondering his next move. "I exercise until I pass out. You?"

"Same." She glanced at his hands, the knuckles still raw from his altercation with her wall. "Unless I'm lying on the couch breathing into a paper bag."

He made his move, and she followed quickly by pushing another pawn forward.

"This 'normal conversation' thing isn't working, is it?" she asked.

"Nope." He slid his queen diagonally across the board.

"Should we talk about the case?"

"Okay then." He focused his still, gray eyes on her. "You've had some time with the files from Arkansas and Colorado. Are they our guy?"

She put the pawn she'd been about to move back down in its original position. "Yes."

He sat back and tugged off his UCLA sweatshirt, revealing a black T-shirt underneath. "I assume that answer has something to do with the signature you were talking about?" He tossed the sweatshirt in the general direction of one of the chairs in front of her desk. It missed.

"Exactly," she said, her eyes darting to the puddle of gray material on the floor.

"Tell me."

"Okay. The two murders had a lot in common with the last homicide." Her words tapered off, and she craned her head to look at his abandoned sweatshirt once more. It was just sitting there. Mocking her.

Get FREE BOOKS and a FREE GIFT when you play the...

LAS VEGAS GAME

*Just scratch off
the gold box with a coin.
Then check below to see
the gifts you get!*

YES! I have scratched off the gold Box. Please send me my **2 FREE BOOKS** and **gift for which I qualify.** I understand that I am under no obligation to purchase any books as explained on the back of this card.

382 HDL DVEP   182 HDL DVE5

FIRST NAME	LAST NAME

ADDRESS

APT.#	CITY

STATE/PROV.	ZIP/POSTAL CODE

(H-I-01/04)

▼ DETACH AND MAIL CARD TODAY! ▼

The Harlequin Reader Service® — Here's how it works:

BUSINESS REPLY MAIL
FIRST-CLASS MAIL   PERMIT NO. 717-003   BUFFALO, NY

POSTAGE WILL BE PAID BY ADDRESSEE

HARLEQUIN READER SERVICE
3010 WALDEN AVE
PO BOX 1867
BUFFALO NY 14240-9952

NO POSTAGE
NECESSARY
IF MAILED
IN THE
UNITED STATES

If offer card is missing write to: Harlequin Reader Service, 3010 Walden Ave., P.O. Box 1867, Buffalo NY 14240-1867

"How so?" he prompted. She could have sworn she heard laughter in his voice.

"Hang on." Pushing herself away from the table, Maggie got up and scooped up the offending garment. She folded it and laid it on top of her neat desk, patting it into place, until its sides were evenly parallel with the desk's edges. Satisfied, she walked back and sat down. "As soon as he revealed himself, the killer subdued all three with a blow to the head or the use of debilitating drugs like chloroform. They were each bound with fishing line to further ensure their submission. The bodies all showed extensive signs of pre- and postmortem picquerism, or being stabbed and cut with a knife. What are you doing?"

He'd leaned over the top of the table, staring intently at the neat row of black chess pieces she'd captured from him. He flicked his forefinger, toppling two pawns and that offending bishop in rapid succession. With a small smile on his lips, he sat back. "You were saying?"

"Autopsy reports revealed that they'd been asphyxiated and revived numerous times before death. And the victims were all stripped naked and their bodies were posed after death."

He started laughing.

Unbelievable. The first time she'd ever heard Billy laugh, and it was at a detailed description of a homicide. And she'd let this man into her house. "Did I mention that being amused by the habits of a serial killer is a little frightening, not to mention *psy-*

chotic?'' And so was thinking that he had a nice laugh.

"No, wait. Look." Still smiling, he gestured toward her side of the board.

The pieces he'd toppled were all upright once more, precisely in line with the others he'd left standing. She hadn't even realized she'd picked them up. "And your point is?"

With a wicked gleam in his eyes, he simply reached over and flicked at a pawn in the center of her line. It toppled and rolled toward the edge of the table, stopping just short of falling off the edge. "Just an experiment," he said.

Maggie frowned and moved a piece of hers on the board.

"So the bodies were all posed after death," he said. "Go on."

"As I was saying..." She glared in a benevolent way at him. "Just one of those elements—bondage, torture, picquerism, and posing—is rare enough."

"Sure," Billy shrugged and moved the black queen forward. "Most homicides are committed in the heat of the moment. The perp kills out of anger or to achieve a goal, like speeding up an inheritance. He or she usually doesn't enjoy it."

"Exactly," she said, reaching for the pawn Billy had knocked over earlier. He cleared his throat pointedly, and she snatched her hand away. "Plus, all the victims are smart, successful women. Our guy is obviously threatened by strong women."

"So he proves he's a man by exercising the ultimate form of control over these women," he said.

Maggie nodded. "The power of life and death."

Billy swore quietly, the first show of overt emotion she'd seen from him since she'd held him after he came home from Gina Markson's murder scene. "I've heard people refer to something called 'the Madonna complex....'"

"That usually refers to the killer's attitude toward women who are sexually aggressive. He uses their overt sexuality to justify using brute violence against them—to 'teach them a lesson,' so to speak." Maggie felt a twinge of pain in her fingers, and when she looked down, she saw she had picked the cuticles on her left thumb and middle finger raw, without even noticing she was doing it. "In the Surgeon's case, he may be interpreting the women's strength and outspokenness as overt sexuality. My guess, though, is that the women remind him of some woman in his past whom he perceives has wronged him. He's reenacting the same kill, over and over."

"But there's something different about the way he sees you."

She brought her abused thumb to her mouth and blew on it. "There are some similarities. I'm an expert in my field, so he may perceive me as intelligent and outspoken." Her eyes darted briefly to the toppled pawn. "Then, there's the added bonus in that my books are about criminals just like him. If he kills me, he thinks that'll make him more famous than he already is."

"Bigger than Bundy, Dahmer, Gacy," Billy said grimly.

"Pretty much." Finally, the impulse proved irresistible, and Maggie picked up the offending pawn, standing it upright with the other captured pieces. She tapped at it, until you could have measured it against the other pieces in the line with a ruler.

He raised an eyebrow at her.

"So I like order," she said lamely. "I like order in my house."

The faint smile that had been playing on his lips died. "It's an illusion, Mags."

She felt her shoulders slump. "I know." Her forefinger worked furiously at the raw cuticle around her thumbnail. Billy reached across the table and closed his hand around hers, stopping her.

"I won't let him get to you, Mags. I promise you."

Maggie blinked, startled. When he looked at her like that, she could almost believe him. "He won't stop. Not until one of us is dead. I mean, he wants immortality."

"And, like you said, he wants to prove he's smarter than you. Sounds like our guy has ego issues."

"Oh!" Maggie shoved back in her chair. She reached up and tapped herself on the forehead, trying to jar the thought that eluded her into place. "Of course. How could I be such an idiot?"

Billy narrowed his eyes.

She twirled her hand at the wrist, until the words she was searching for finally came to her. "Ego issues. He likes to play games with the police, insert himself into the investigation, stuff like that. We can use that.''

"So, the memorial service for Gina Markson on Wednesday,'' Billy said, staying right with her even though homicide wasn't his beat. "You think he'd show up?''

"If we can get it in the papers. Can we?'' Gina's family had already held her funeral—today, if Maggie remembered correctly. But the students at the Institute of International Studies were putting together an all-school memorial service for Gina, and it would take place in exactly four days. She rose and made her way to the phone on her immaculate desk.

Billy whipped out his omnipresent cell phone. "I'm on it. I know some reporters with the *Chronicle,* and I bet Brentwood and Borkowski have an ally in the local press.''

"They can help us plan, too,'' Maggie said as she watched him hit his speed dial. "Let's just hope this guy accepts our invitation.''

Chapter Eight

The afternoon before Gina Markson's memorial service, Maggie sat in her office window seat, wrapped in a worn quilt her grandmother had made her, and stared at the sea. A sharp, cool wind blowing in from the west rippled across the Pacific, stirring up whitecaps and making the water spray high into the air when it hit the jagged rocks along the shoreline. Not that the water was calm even when there was no wind. The ocean near most of Monterey Peninsula was always foaming, moving, crashing. Almost monthly, you heard news reports of someone falling into the deep pools near some areas of the shoreline, never to be seen again. And though some intrepid swimmers took their surfboards out at times, surfing even the calmest stretches of water was dangerous, due to the many riptides and undertows.

It had been fun, though.

Maggie pulled the quilt tighter around herself. Fun. It wasn't fun being locked inside your house for eighteen months, fearing a horrible death at the hands of a maniac. But in her house she remained, scared out of her mind. Literally.

Her heart thundered in her chest at the sound of a key scraping in the front door lock. Billy. It's just Billy, she told herself, back from running some errands right when he said he'd be. She forced herself to remain seated like a normal person, instead of lunging for the nearest weapon the way she wanted to.

As soon as he stepped in the door, he called out his presence, and her pulse returned to normal. They hadn't done much more than work and continue the longest game of chess she'd ever played, but she felt comfortable with him in her house. Sometimes, on the rarest and quietest of moments, she even felt relaxed.

Weird.

Shrugging the quilt off her shoulders, she spun around to face the door, just as Billy walked into the room. The gold hoop in his left ear glinted in the fading sunlight, and the black Lakers sweatshirt he wore with his jeans brought out the ever-present five-o'clock shadow on his face. When she'd first met him, she'd thought he had to work to get his stubble that perfect, but it turned out he just hated shaving.

She smiled hello at him, and then an incredible aroma coming from the bags he carried hit her square in the hunger pangs. "Oh. My. God. Don't tell me you went to Mariposa."

Raising one dark eyebrow at her—a trick she couldn't mimic even if she practiced in the mirror—he set the white plastic bags on her desk and flipped them around so the logo on them faced her. An orange butterfly fluttered in between script letters that did indeed spell out Mariposa, the name of the excellent and relatively undiscovered Cuban restaurant half a mile from her house.

She closed her eyes and inhaled deeply, reveling in the smells of lime-marinated chicken, *arroz con frijoles negros,* and maybe, if her nose wasn't playing tricks on her, fried *platanos.* "Wow. I haven't had Mariposa in months." She didn't like to bother Adriana with picking up take-out orders as well as Maggie's groceries and mail. "I don't suppose you have caramel flan in there?"

Billy reached inside one bag and pulled out a plastic container, which he opened. Inside was one perfect dome-shaped custard with dark-brown caramel sauce dripping down the sides.

"Ohhh," Maggie said, unable to keep the reverence out of her voice.

Billy laughed. "You look like I just gave you a four-carat diamond."

"Diamond, schmiamond," she scoffed, clutching the container with both hands. "Do you have any idea how rare perfect flan is? Especially in a portion size that isn't made for mice? Mariposa's flan is—" She gestured lamely. "There are no words."

"So are you going to let me pry that away and take it to the dining room," he asked, "or am I running the risk of serious injury just by mentioning it?"

She held out the container. "No, I trust you."

He reached out to take it from her, his hands overlapping hers—by accident or by design, she didn't know. She didn't care.

Time stopped.

The comfort she'd felt in Billy Corrigan's presence during the last four days was replaced by something different, something more. Attraction wrapped around her like a cloud of incense, seductive, heady, dangerous. She raised her head and met his eyes, which had turned from ice-gray to the color of a mountain lake. Then her gaze went to his mouth.

He took his hands away. She blinked and stepped back.

"So." Maggie ducked her head to examine the other containers. "What else did you bring?"

"Lime chicken, a couple of movies."

"Dinner and a movie," she murmured.

Billy shrugged. "I thought you should have one normal night before tomorrow." He put the flan container into one of the bags and picked it up. "Things are going to get crazy."

Then he moved through the doorway and disappeared into the dining room, leaving her alone for a moment in the office to wonder what had just happened between them.

THE NEXT DAY, a few hours before Gina Markson's memorial service would start, Maggie sat in her office chair talking to her computer screen. "Based on his past actions and similar cases I've studied, the odds are with us that the Surgeon will show up at the auditorium, especially now that the *County Herald* made it yesterday's front-page story.'' Thanks to Billy's quick technical fix, the entire Monterey PD task force—except Billy and James Brentwood, who were with her—could see and hear her in the briefing room at the station. All that, and she didn't have to leave the comfort of her own home. ''This kind of killer takes great pleasure in seeing the aftereffects of his murders.''

She couldn't see the task force or the briefing room—the camera system only went one way. But she could hear those closest to the microphone over her PC's speakers. The whole conversation was kept completely secure by Billy's own encryption programs.

Borkowski's businesslike voice, sounding as though it was being broadcast live from Neptune, crackled over the connection: ''Officer Hayden wants to know how we'll be able to spot him.''

''It's not going to be easy,'' Maggie admitted, grabbing a tissue from the box on her desk and wiping off the screen. She stopped and tossed the tissue in the trash when she remembered the entire task force could see her. ''He's gotten away with at least eleven murders—this is a guy who blends in with his surroundings. The Surgeon isn't the social chameleon Ted Bundy was, so if he's there, he'll be hanging quietly on the sidelines. We're setting up a table near the main exit to the auditorium, where people can sign a form to volunteer for a campus safety committee.''

''Detective Brentwood and I will be joining the Institute's Dean of Students behind that table,'' Borkowski interjected. "Our hope is that the Surgeon will be one of our happy little volunteers."

"The form is just the kind of thing he'd sign," Maggie said, anticipating the next question, "whether with his real name or, most likely, a pseudonym, to thumb his nose at us."

"Can you explain why you think this will work?" Borkowski's voice sounded tinny. Not the best connection in the world, but then again, Billy had managed to put it together without the bells and whistles the FBI would have supplied. Maggie had been told her face was being projected from the computer to a large screen in the briefing room, helping the task force to see her as a real person, and a real expert on their side. It sounded awfully *Star Trek* to Maggie, but Borkowski and Brentwood apparently thought it was a good idea.

"He's written letters and called prominent media and law-enforcement personnel in the past. The Surgeon likes to taunt the people who are looking for him." She didn't mention that in New Orleans, she had been on the receiving end of most of his phone calls and letters. "On one occasion, he told us he was at a funeral and walked right up to the police attending the service. He'll be there. And this time, we'll be ready." She hoped. Oh, how she hoped.

At that point, Borkowski took over the rest of the briefing. She, Brentwood and six MPD detectives on the scene would stand in predetermined locations in the auditorium—right next to several hidden cameras. At Maggie's instruction, they'd eliminate the women who signed up, as well as those with physical conditions that would prevent them from carrying out multiple homicides across state lines. The rest would form the body of their first list of suspects, each of whom would have to be investigated and eliminated. Or maybe, if they were lucky, today would be the day they'd get the major break in the case everyone was praying for.

"Okay, people," Borkowski said to the task force and assorted personnel. "Let's get it done."

Maggie sat back in her chair and removed the headset, tossing it on top of her desk with a clatter. Grabbing an Angels ball cap from the coat rack behind her, she dropped it unceremoniously over the small dome-shaped Web cam. She closed all the windows on her computer screen, hoping that the actions shut down the Web camera. But she didn't remove the baseball cap, just as a precaution—she didn't want to be her own Internet reality show if she could help it.

With a sigh, she got up and headed into the kitchen. Billy stood next to her kitchen counter, his smooth-shaven chin tilted upward while James Brentwood hooked a long-range transmitter to his shirt collar. The six key police detectives, as well as Brentwood and Borkowski, would wear the transmitters, allowing them to stay in contact with each other and with Maggie. Two officers would stay behind and guard her door.

With his wire in place, Brentwood excused himself and headed outside. Maggie couldn't quite believe the whole operation would go down without her there.

She was almost tempted to try going outside again, but she knew that wasn't such a good idea. The last thing she needed was to make a fool of herself in front of Billy and the detective just after she'd finally managed to re-establish some of her former credibility. *Time to hold it together, Reyes.*

The decision didn't make her feel any better about sending Billy in her place. Her gut twisted as she watched him fasten the buttons on the cuffs of his crisp, dark-gray dress shirt. His earring was gone. He looked like an ordinary man dressed in an ordinary, though well-tailored suit. His thick brown hair, spike-free today, was gelled into a conservative side-part. But she knew better. Today was so far from ordinary. Part of her hoped she was wrong, and the day would go by uneventfully. Part of her wanted him to stay with her, safe, even though she knew he wouldn't stay, even if she asked. Even if she begged.

Without stopping to ponder the wisdom of her action, Maggie reached for the sapphire-blue silk tie that lay draped over the top of one of the kitchen chairs.

"Need help with this?" she asked with forced casualness, looping the tie across her palm without bothering to wait for his answer.

He glanced at her without raising his head from his cuffs, the movement causing a gelled piece of hair to fall onto his forehead in a manner she found unexpectedly charming. With his dark, pressed trousers and polished black shoes, he looked as though he was about to depart for a day's work at the stock exchange, not heading for a meeting with one of the country's most vicious serial killers. The thought made her ache for him.

She waited for him to finish tucking in his shirt, then looped the tie over his head. Her fingers brushed the warm skin of his neck as she tucked the strip of silk underneath his collar. "Be careful, okay?" she said, trying desperately to keep her tone light. "I don't think I can sleep anymore without you snoring in the next room."

He raised his chin, allowing her to tighten the knot at his throat. "I don't snore."

She scoffed at that. "Then someone's obviously been operating a meat grinder in the spare room while you're sleeping, because there's some hideous noise coming from in there, and it started when you moved in, bud." The knot in place, Maggie focused on pulling the ends of the tie into a straight line over the row of buttons on his shirt. "I don't want you to go," she said suddenly, before she could stop herself.

His body went completely still. She could have sworn he'd even stopped breathing for a moment. "I'll be careful," he finally said, his voice a low rumble inside his chest.

"Will you?" She stared at the buttons on his shirt-front, afraid to look at him. "Your need for vengeance scares me, Billy."

"It scares me, too, sometimes," he admitted softly.

Leaning forward, she kissed his battered knuckles, reveling in the feel of his warm skin under her lips, knowing that she'd regret the impulse later. "I want you away from here," she whispered into his fingers.

"Away from me. Get out of this world, Billy, before it eats you alive."

His hand flexed slightly, but otherwise, he didn't move. "I'm not leaving you, Mags," he said, his voice a touch more hoarse than it had been before.

"I wish you would," she said, finally looking up at his face.

With slow, deliberate movements, he reached out to toy with a lock of her hair, a faraway look in his gray eyes. "I know." And somehow, without her knowing who moved first, their faces were inches apart, his mouth so close to hers, she could feel his breath on her face.

She wanted him. It shocked her, even as she came close to losing herself in the emotion. She was so conscious of the beating of his heart, the feel of his broad shoulders beneath her hands, the way his breathing had changed as soon as he held her in his arms. Most of all, she was conscious of feeling something for him that she never should have allowed to take root.

"Billy—" she gasped, wishing he would leave, but wanting him to stay even more. She plunged one hand into the soft thickness of his dark hair.

"This is a bad idea, Mags," he whispered against her mouth. "On so many levels." The warning made her instinctively jerk away, but he placed one hand on the small of her back and pulled her against his lean, hard body.

"But I never said you should stop." He brushed

his mouth against hers with the lightest of touches, questioning, seeking, and unbelievably sexy.

Stop. They really should stop. Maggie knew it, but somehow she just couldn't make her body comply. Standing on tiptoe, she gripped the tie she'd just straightened and pulled him even closer, thinking about nothing else other than deepening the kiss. It didn't take much. Billy tugged the clip that held her ponytail out of her hair, causing it to rain down her shoulders in a cascade of curls. He growled softly and plunged his hands into her thick hair, then cupped the back of her head as his mouth moved expertly against hers. And then all she could think about was him.

For a few heady seconds, Maggie let herself be a normal woman being kissed by a good-looking man who was interested in her. And then the fingertips she skimmed down his spine encountered the gun tucked into an inner pants holster hidden in the small of his back.

They were not normal. She was not normal. Maybe she never would be again.

"Please." She pulled her face away from his in a burst of sheer willpower. "I can't."

Before she could even blink, Billy moved to the other side of the kitchen, putting the wood-and-steel island between them. His chest heaved with each breath he took, and his gray eyes were smoky with tension. With wanting her.

"I shouldn't," he said, his voice calm, deep, belying the fire in his eyes and the air between them. "Doesn't mean I always do what I should."

She gripped the edge of the counter, hoping it would keep her grounded, keep her from making a fool of herself and reaching for him again. "I'm sorry. I kept touching you. I—" She clenched her hands in frustration, her nails scraping along the wood. "I'd be using you, Billy. I'm scared, and I'm needy, and I've been alone for a long time. I can't do this."

He leaned his body against the kitchen table, folding his arms and focusing entirely on her. "Maybe you're too hard on yourself," he said.

"How can I not be?" She leaned forward to rest her elbows on the counter, tracing a small scratch on its surface with one hand. "I'm sick and I need to get better. And pulling you into my twisted world before that happens isn't going to do you any good."

"Why don't you let me be the judge of that?"

She felt a slight prickling behind her eyes and hoped to heaven she wouldn't start crying. Too much emotion intruding into her safe, narrow world. Too much for her to handle in one day. "It's not good for me, either."

He didn't respond, and when she glanced at him, she saw his head was bowed and his eyes were closed. Then, his eyes snapped open, the rest of his features schooled themselves into perfect, shuttered blankness. He grabbed his suit coat from a chair it had been draped across and shrugged into it. She moved slowly around the island to stand before him, fighting the urge to straighten his tie and touch him one last time.

He touched her first. He reached into the inside

pocket of the jacket and pulled out a small headset. Tucking her hair out of the way, he hooked the headset over her right ear. His touch made her ache. His gentleness made her feel like crying.

Then he took his hands away and tapped a wireless ear plant tucked inside his ear. "A little more sophisticated than my cell phone," he said, all business now. "There are eight MPD detectives, including Brentwood and Borkowski, who'll be wearing these. We'll be able to hear everything you say into your headset. And these…" He pointed to a tiny pin in the shape of an American flag tacked to his lapel. "These have a small microphone in them, so we can talk back to you, and to each other on a special tactical channel. I'll be the one describing the scene to you—everyone else has been instructed to keep the connection as clear as possible. If we get disconnected, call the MPD non-emergency line and ask to be patched through to Borkowski or Brentwood."

"Thanks." They were back to business, as if the kiss had never happened, and she wasn't sure if she liked it. She watched as he hid another small gun in his ankle holster, tucked the flat wallet with his badge into the inner breast pocket of his black suit jacket. Since he wasn't the type to own many suits, she found herself imagining the last time he'd worn this one— perhaps at Jenna's funeral, as he'd watched the first shovelful of dirt fall on the wooden box that held his sister.

He started toward the door, and she found herself blurting "be careful" once more.

He turned one corner of his mouth upward in that enigmatic half-smile of his. "I just want things to be good for you, Mags," he said. And then once again, he left her alone in the house she couldn't escape.

Maggie walked into her office and sat down in front of the chessboard, where her pieces and Billy's sat frozen, waiting for the game to continue. With a slow, deliberate movement, she pushed her queen forward. And then she waited for Billy to come home and make his next move.

STUDENTS AND FACULTY poured into the Irvine Auditorium, filling almost all 400 of the theater's velvet-covered seats. It wasn't that all of them knew Gina Markson personally; rather, they came out of a sense of solidarity and a need to do something to give themselves a sense of control over their situation, even if it was just an illusion.

Detectives Brentwood and Borkowski stood behind a table near the entrance, which featured three clipboards holding sign-up sheets for members of an ad hoc advisory committee on campus safety. Beside them stood Rita Gentrey, the Monterey Institute of International Studies dean of students. The petite blonde in a sturdy navy blue suit was doing almost too good of a job reining in passersby and coaxing them to add their names, addresses and phone numbers—the list was growing huge.

Billy walked around the theater, keeping his stride casual as he took in every entrance and exit the theater had. "O'Donnell and Moreno are at the backstage entrances, within visual range of each other,'' he said in the general direction of the flag pin on his lapel, taking care to move his lips as little as possible. ''Cardenas and Ramirez are standing near the stage at the southeast exit.'' He passed the front of the stage and continued up the second aisle that stretched from the auditorium's front to its rear. ''Hayes and Lockwood have the front of the place.'' They were dressed in the blue uniforms of campus security, complete with staticky radios and large batons strapped to their utility belts. ''And about twenty officers and campus security personnel are stationed randomly in the auditorium.''

''Great. And Brentwood and Borkowski?'' Maggie responded through the earphone he was wearing.

''Their table is just to the right of the main doors on the north side of the theater. The dean of students is with them.'' Billy watched as the dean blocked the path of two young women and started her campus safety committee pitch. Obviously someone thought the committee was more than just a way to trap Gina's killer. ''So far, Brentwood says our safety committee is mostly women. We've had exactly five men sign up. One had a knee brace, two were with their girlfriends, and two were professors with daughters who live near campus.''

''Any impressions?'' Maggie said. Since they were on the same frequency the eight MPD detectives were using to talk to each other, he and Maggie kept their comments as brief as possible.

''I'd scratch the professors. They've been teaching

here for years, and the students I've talked to say they're both very popular, well-spoken men.''

"Probably not our guy," Maggie agreed. "How about the knee brace and the two with girlfriends?"

"I've got my eye on knee brace. Could be a fake. He's quiet, sullen, and arrived alone. Looks to be about twenty-four or so."

"Young guy. Gut feeling?"

"The way he's favoring his knee looks legit. Scrawny enough that at least one of the girls should have been able to get away from him." Jenna would have kicked the snot out of him, Billy thought, then pushed the image of his sister away. Right now was no time to think about Jenna.

"Remember, this guy ambushes from behind. He doesn't have to be that powerful," Maggie cautioned.

Billy zeroed in on the guy with the brace, who'd chosen an aisle seat two rows from the top. "He gave Borkowski a name and contact info, though. We'll check him out."

Billy leaned against a large steel support pole that reached into the rafters and scanned the crowd milling about the auditorium. Most of them stood in groups of twos and threes, talking in low whispers. Hundreds of faces, and one could belong to the man who'd killed his sister. But which one?

"Keep watching him," Maggie said. "And remember to get as much as you can from anyone who comes forward with 'helpful' information."

"Will do." The theater lights blinked on and off, signaling the crowd to find their seats. The president of the university, a heavyset man with twinkling eyes and almost no hair, climbed the stairs to take his place behind the podium, shuffling a handful of papers as he waited for the attendees to find their places.

Within minutes, everyone was seated and the president began to speak. "Good afternoon, ladies and gentleman. Today, we come together to remember a young woman who was not only one of our finest students, but a friend, mentor and example to many." It sounded nearly identical to the comments the president of Tulane had made at a similar service for Jenna.

With some effort to ignore the sudden tightness in his throat, Billy tuned the man's words out and continued to scrutinize the audience. The boy with the knee brace looked slightly bored, while the two professors who had signed the campus safety sheet were both listening intently. The room itself was silent, except for the occasional sniffle or sigh. Gina Markson had had a lot of friends.

Brentwood and Borkowski were still at their table, taking signatures from the few stragglers who had come in late. Cardenas and Ramirez stood at the front of the theater, watching the crowd with hawklike attention.

He couldn't see Hayes and Lockwood, though he assumed they were in the foyer.

Too many faces. Too little information.

Where are you, you son of a bitch?

Maybe Maggie was wrong. She'd been out of the game for a long time. Maybe the Surgeon was out stalking his next victim, planning his next kill. Maybe they were wasting their time.

But dammit, he'd brought her into the case. Doubting her now wouldn't do anything but lower his guard. If the Surgeon did show, Billy would be ready.

Ready for what? his inner voice demanded. *What will you do when you find him?*

Kill him.

He felt cold, a peculiar kind of cold that started from the inside and worked its way out. The hair on his arms and the back of his neck stood at attention, and with every beat of his heart, he felt as if his body was turning to brittle ice.

Time slowed to a crawl. The sounds around him dimmed as if he'd suddenly plunged underwater, but the sights went into sharp focus. The president at the podium. Cardenas and Ramirez shifting from foot to foot. The boy with the knee brace scratching his leg. The dean of students making her way to the stage. The lights burning brightly on the crowd in their seats.

He could hear his heartbeat in his ears.

Someone was watching him.

"He's here," he said aloud.

Maggie's response was instant. "Where?"

Borkowski's head snapped around.

Brentwood put his hand on his gun and backed away from the table. Cardenas and Ramirez stopped shifting.

"I can feel it," he said.

The detectives in the room didn't relax at his revelation. They knew how important intuition could be to some in their field, and they all knew better than to scoff. As far as they were concerned, Gina Markson's murderer was in that very room, watching them. Now they just had to find him.

"Cardenas and Ramirez, stay where you are," he heard Borkowski say through the wire. "O'Donnell and Moreno, report in."

As the two detectives responded, Billy moved toward the edge of the crowd and searched the sea of faces, focusing a split-second's worth of attention on every person he could take in. Was it the skinny guy standing in the back of the theater? The scruffy man in his thirties standing in the doorway looking bored? The professorial type in the aisle seat scowling at the stage?

"Hayes and Lockwood, report in," Borkowski said. She and Brentwood had fanned out and were making their way to one of the theater's side entrances.

Billy locked eyes with a man who stood across the auditorium from him. Smiling.

He was built like a fire hydrant, with a thick neck, broad shoulders, and a military precision haircut. His clothing was nondescript—a dark-green cotton jacket, jeans, a dirty white T-shirt. Thanks to the overhead lighting, the man's eyes were hidden in shadow. And he was fondling something he held close to his flat stomach.

A sudden violence overtook him, and Billy wanted to charge across the room and wipe that smile off the man's face with his bare hands. Remaining where he was took all of his control and left him shaking in the attempt. He reached into the pocket of his suit jacket and pulled out a pair of mini-binoculars.

"Hayes and Lockwood, report in," Borkowski repeated.

Billy aimed the binoculars at the man's hands, the hands that had killed his sister. The hands that wouldn't be enough to save him once Billy crossed the room. "I've spotted a suspect, early 30s, dark-green jacket. Directly across the room from where I'm standing. He's holding something," he reported. He adjusted the focus and saw that the man was rubbing the piece of fabric that just barely stuck out of his jacket pocket. It was blue.

Like Gina Markson's shirt.

"Hayes and Lockwood," Borkowski called over the connection, her voice grown louder with urgency. The detectives never interrupted each other, unless it was urgent. As in two detectives gone missing. "Brentwood and Borkowski have spotted suspect. Stand by, Agent Corrigan."

"Billy?" Maggie interjected into the drawn-out pause that followed.

Billy whipped the binoculars up to the man's face. Still smiling, the man mouthed something it took Billy only a few tenths of a second to decipher.

How's your sister?

"Billy? Answer me."

"Hayes and Lockwood, report in!" Borkowski barked.

"Billy, oh, God."

"CARDENAS, RAMIREZ, I need you near the entrance *now*," Borkowski's voice cut sharply into the silence over the headset Maggie wore. "Agent Corrigan just exited through the main rear doors in pursuit of an unknown subject. Brentwood and I are directly behind him." There was a moment of static, and then: "Gather all personnel and secure the exits. And find Hayes and Lockwood."

Maggie's fist crashed onto her desk, sending papers and photos flying. Damn the man for being such a hothead. Wanting to scream in frustration, Maggie gripped the flexible microphone end of the headset and brought it as close to her mouth as it would go. She didn't want Billy to miss a word of what she was about to say.

"Agent Corrigan, do not, I repeat, do not go after the unsub without backup," she said, using the standard abbreviation for "unknown subject." "You know better."

Nothing.

"Billy, answer me. Where are you?"

Still nothing.

Oh God, ohgodohgod. Please let nothing have happened to him, the stubborn, impulsive fool.

"I can hear Brentwood and Borkowski behind me," Billy's voice called over the connection. "I'm turning right at the coat check area." Maggie nearly collapsed with relief at the sound. He was a little breathless, meaning he was running.

"Corrigan, where is the unsub?" Borkowski snapped over the line.

"About fifteen paces ahead of me. We're heading into the sidestage hallways."

Maggie went to the blueprint of the Irvine Auditorium that lay spread out on her desk. It was like a labyrinth. And that meant it was deadly.

Too many shadows. Too many places to hide.

"Agent Corrigan, we are right behind you. O'Donnell, Moreno," Borkowski called to the two detectives positioned behind the stage, "I want you to move around back and head the unsub off. Reyes?"

"O'Donnell, Moreno, go to the backstage area and exit through the door on your left," Maggie said at Borkowski's prompt, tracing a finger along the blueprint as she scanned a possible route for the two detectives. "Go forward until you reach a T-intersection in the hall and take a left. Continue in that direction until you meet up with Agent Corrigan or hear him down one of the side corridors."

She only hoped they'd get there soon enough.

"And watch your backs," she said.

The line grew quiet, with only the sounds of static and running footsteps on bare polished floors giving Maggie any clue as to what was going on. She paced near her desk, listening intently as she waited. God, she hated waiting.

What if you've killed him, Maggie? What if he dies because of you? What if they all do?

She spun around, feeling as though the walls that

she used to find so comforting were closing in on her. Her next breath came out as a gasp, as she choked on the urge to call out his name over the headset until he answered. Oh, Billy.

A loud popping noise burst over the radio. Gunfire. Oh, no.

Maggie nearly collapsed in relief when she heard Billy's strained voice shortly thereafter. "I'm still in pursuit. Borkowski?"

"We lost you in the gunfire, Agent Corrigan. Which way did you turn?"

Billy responded, but the words were unintelligible over a sudden burst of static.

Maggie smacked a palm against the window, watching the waves crash over the rocks.

"Agent Corrigan, please repeat," Borkowski snapped.

Brentwood swore into his headset.

"He's armed," Billy shouted. "I'm—"

Maggie heard a sickening thud come over the wires, then the sound of someone groaning in pain. And then she heard nothing.

"Agent Corrigan?"

Oh, no.

"Man down! We've got a man down!"

"Agent Corrigan?"

"Ma'am, this is O'Donnell," a low-pitched female voice broke into the chaos. "Ma'am, we've found Hayes and Lockwood."

Chapter Nine

Maggie's connection to the police detectives died in a spectacular burst of static. She called the non-emergency line, as Billy had instructed, only to be told they were having technical problems and wouldn't be able to patch her in for at least an hour. In sheer, helpless frustration, Maggie ripped off the headset and threw it across the room.

What have you done, you stupid, selfish woman? She'd sent a broken, grief-driven man into the path of one of the world's most dangerous criminals, just because she wanted an inside view of the investigation. Just so she could look through his eyes and see what was coming for her.

She paced back and forth across the room for what felt like hours, beating back the urge to curl up in a ball and cry. The house that had been her sanctuary now felt like prison.

What if I've killed him? And Hayes and Lockwood?

Stifling a sob with her fist, Maggie whirled around and charged through the office door, down the hallway, past the phone that wouldn't ring.

I've got to get out.

With a flick of her wrist, she shot back the dead-bolt, then undid the security chain. Her hand closed around the doorknob.

I've got to get out.

An image flashed through her mind of the man she'd only known for days: working in her kitchen; watching the ocean from her office with still, gray eyes that had become adept at hiding the loss he'd suffered; scooping her up in his arms when the fear of a nameless, faceless killer became too much. And she wondered if she'd sent him to his death.

Get out.

Stumbling forward, she crossed the threshold to the porch. She had to get to him. She owed him that much. Two more steps, and she had wrapped her arms around the support column near the small stairs to her front door. She could do this. She would find him.

Late-morning fog seeped through the grove of cypress and oak trees across the street, and she could hear the sound of the crashing ocean behind her. Without warning, the whole scene undulated before her eyes, as if it were about to start spinning around her. She flicked her gaze to the steps in front of her, still gripping the column.

Gritting her teeth, she slowly brought one sneakered foot over the edge of the porch, where it hovered over the first step.

Don't look at the sky. Don't look at the trees.

"Come on," she gasped, willing her body to obey her and step forward already. "Come on." Closing her eyes, she pulled her left hand away from the column, swinging her arm out in front of her. Left with nothing to hold on to, her fingers involuntarily closed over cool morning air.

She opened her eyes, and the world tilted on its axis. The hand still clinging to the column scrabbled for a stronger purchase, and she stumbled onto the first step almost by accident.

Before she had time to celebrate that first victory, her gaze dropped to the second stair. The thought of going through the same process for every step nearly undid her, but she pushed it firmly out of her head. One at a time. Slowly, focusing on the white tip of her sneaker, she uncurled her arm from around the support column. Her hand skimmed along its wooden surface, nails scraping against the white paint.

Don't look at the sky. Don't look at the trees.

Something darted in and out of her peripheral vision. Although the high-pitched screech it emitted told her the object was nothing but a seagull, it didn't make a bit of difference. Her head shot up, and the cloudy sky began to circle around her. The trees stretched up, up, up, until their twisted branches loomed over her like the fingers of a giant hand. And the wind blew through her with the force of a hurricane.

Vertigo, her mind screamed. It's just an illusion.

But the illusion was powerful, and her will wasn't enough. Bright bursts of light danced in front of her eyes, and she felt her body pitching down, down, down as her vision turned to black.

Oh, God, Billy, I can't do this without you.

"MAGGIE?"

A soft voice floated through the fog that had enveloped her. "Maggie, wake up. *Ay, chica,* I told you not to get involved."

Maggie groaned, batting groggily at the hand shaking her shoulder, but its grip refused to loosen. Caught in the quagmire between sleeping and waking, Maggie shook her head back and forth, mumbling something unintelligible even to her ears.

"Please be all right. James, maybe we should call an ambulance."

At the thought of being forcibly carried out of her house, Maggie jerked awake, her eyes popping open. She turned toward the voice that had pulled her out of blessed oblivion. "Addy?"

"*Ay,* I'm so glad you're okay. We found you face down in the sand outside your house."

Maggie swiped the back of her hand across her eye, stretching the other arm out. "Outside?"

"That's what I said." Adriana bit her lip, peering at her through a pair of rhinestone-studded glasses with clear plastic lenses that probably had no corrective power whatsoever. Her hair was streaked with vivid coral. "What the heck were you doing out there? Not that I don't applaud the effort, but couldn't you wait until someone was here in case you wigged?"

"I didn't wig." Maggie rubbed the bridge of her nose, trying to remember what had happened. "Okay, fine, I wigged. I—'' The memory of her recent past hit her like a blow to the chest. She inhaled sharply and searched behind Adriana for James Brentwood. ''Billy, what's happened to Billy?''

James Brentwood walked past Adriana and sat next to Maggie on the couch. ''He's fine. Nasty concussion, but otherwise he's safe. He's at Community Hospital under observation, but they'll probably release him in a few hours.''

She leaned back against the sofa cushions, feeling suddenly small and lost. ''And Hayes and Lockwood?''

At the mention of the two detectives, Brentwood grew suddenly pale. ''He took them out. Two of our best. I've never seen anything like it.''

Maggie felt her hands start to shake. ''Took them out?''

Brentwood waved a hand at her, as if to cut off the train of thought he knew she was following. ''They're alive,'' he said, ''but he knocked them both out cold. Hayes sustained some cracked ribs, and Lockwood's jaw is broken.'' His shoulders slumped and his eyes grew unfocused as he shook his head. ''How did that happen?''

Maggie covered her hand with her mouth, trying to think past her shock. ''I don't know,'' she said through her fingers. ''We always thought the reason he incapacitated his victims was insecurity. He felt inadequate, physically and/or mentally, so he had to take them down using surprise or sudden force.''

''But he's strong enough to take on two experienced detectives at once? How the hell did he do that?''

Behind him, Addy flinched, obviously unused to hearing the normally cool and collected James Brentwood lose it, even slightly.

Maggie shook her head. ''Training? Someone showed this guy how to take someone down before they can put up a fight, and that's what he does.''

Brentwood clasped his hands together and bent his fingers upward, cracking his knuckles. ''Military?''

''Maybe. That, or worse.'' If he was in the military, it would explain a lot. How the Surgeon was able to slip in and out of neighborhoods, homes, college campuses without being seen. How he walked through locked doors, sealed windows. How he took victims off crowded streets in broad daylight. She knew better than to draw a definite conclusion on only circumstantial evidence, but the fact of the matter was that someone had shown the Surgeon exactly how to be an efficient and deadly killing machine. ''If so, he would probably have a dishonorable discharge on his record,'' she added. ''Sociopaths don't last in group environments.''

''There's something,'' Addy said, obviously hoping the detail might be the missing piece that would lead them to the killer and end their nightmares.

''It's not enough,'' James said, his voice hollow.

''No,'' Maggie agreed. ''What happened in that hallway?''

And James told her how Billy had run after the Surgeon, how Brentwood and Borkowski had followed close behind, dropping to the floor when gunfire rang out. They'd gotten up, only to turn the corner and find that the hallways forked—and they couldn't see Billy or the unsub down any of them.

"We heard Agent Corrigan fall, and through sheer, blind luck, we chose the right hallway and found him." James threw his hands in the air, frustration evident on his rugged features. "But the guy we were chasing was gone. It was like he'd vanished. O'Donnell and Moreno came running up from the backstage area, and they hadn't seen even a sign of him."

Brentwood snapped open the briefcase Maggie hadn't noticed lying at his feet, and pulled out a piece of paper. "Agent Corrigan says the man took his cell phone. And he left the original of this," he said, handing the paper to her.

The note had the same handwriting as the one that had been left at her door. It read, "S12 M0."

"He's still keeping score," Adriana murmured, wrapping her hand over James's shoulder to give or receive comfort, possibly both.

"But it doesn't make sense." Maggie waved the photocopy in the air. "Gina Markson was the eleventh victim, not the twelfth."

"Unless he meant for Billy to be the twelfth and we caught up to him in time."

Maggie frowned, pondering the thought for a moment. "I don't know. His focus is women—something happened in his past that makes him hate women, in a way that goes far beyond what you and

I would call hate. If he attacks men, he won't get the same sense of satisfaction." She shook her head. "I don't think he meant to kill Billy. He was just the messenger."

"Then the 12 is his warning that there will be a twelfth victim, and soon," Brentwood said.

The three of them stared at each other. "I hate this job sometimes," Brentwood muttered. He rose, taking the photocopy back from Maggie. "I'm posting guards outside your door tonight. I'll be back as soon as I can to introduce you to Officers Cartwright and Mason."

But Maggie barely heard him, so intent was she on one word that had fallen from his lips.

Soon.

HER FRONT DOOR *swung open, and Billy stood in the doorway, silhouetted against the brilliant sunlight streaming from behind him into her foyer. The ceramic tiles of her front hallway sparkled as she practically ran across them, a potent relief making her forget caution.*

She threw her arms around him and buried her face against his neck. "I can't believe you're here. I'm so glad to see you," she said, her words muffled.

"It's okay, Magdalena," he murmured into her hair as his broad hands stroked her back. "I've got you. I'll always get you."

"You will," she said. He kissed her then, just a light brush of his lips on hers. His mouth felt cold, colder than she'd remembered.

He smiled and swung her up into his arms, carrying her through the doorway and into the world outside.

"I don't remember the sky being so bright," she said, as they walked through the yard, past the stand of trees that had so terrified her before. Now, in the streaming yellow sunlight, she couldn't remember why she'd ever been scared of them. They were just trees.

They walked on, with him carrying her as if she were light as gossamer, around the house and down the sand to the edge of the ocean she loved. He climbed one of the many black, jagged rocks that dotted the shore.

When they reached the top, she looked down into the small inlet created by a cluster of the rocks. The water surged and foamed beneath them, looking deep and angry and bottomless.

"I could make you disappear," he said, holding her over the water. She laughed at him, despite the ominous meaning of his words.

"I could make you live forever," she responded, cupping her hand against his rough, stubbled cheek. It felt smooth, for some reason.

He put her on the ground then, and as soon as her feet touched the rock, her legs grew suddenly rubbery. They bent and twisted in all directions, as if she were a marionette whose strings were too slack. "What's happening to me?" she asked.

"Why don't you run, Maggie?"

She stared at him, horrified that he would say such a thing, but the sunlight was too bright, and trying to focus on his face made her eyes hurt. She looked away. "How could you ask me that?"

"Where are your guns, Maggie? Where are your guards?" he murmured. "Where is your safe little haven now?"

"I'm always safe near water," she said. But then he waved a hand at her, and her blouse tore in two, falling away from her shoulders. Red, angry marks slashed across her wrist, biting into her skin with a sharp, sudden pain. Panic seized her with cold, pointed fingers, and she knew she had to get away from him. "I need to get out of here," she moaned, struggling against some unseen force that wouldn't allow her to rise. "I need to get out."

The sun ducked behind a cloud, and she saw that Billy's face wasn't really Billy's at all, but some other man's whom she didn't recognize.

The man who wasn't Billy smiled at her, and then she knew him—knew him with a certainty that made her blood run cold.

"You only run from what you can't see," he said.

With a start, Maggie shot into a sitting position, her heart hammering in her ears. The blankets of her bed fell down around her waist. Bed. She was in bed. It was only a dream.

She blinked rapidly, her eyes gummy from sleep. Being extremely myopic without her contact lenses, she couldn't see much further than just past the end of her nose. The rest of the room was a blur of dark and darker areas, illuminated only by the red, glowing blur of a battery-powered alarm clock. She reached for it and pulled it close to her face—3:17 a.m.

She put the clock down and rubbed her face with the palms of both hands. James Brentwood and Adriana had left several hours earlier after introducing her, as promised, to the two police officers who were keeping watch outside her door. They must've made a noise that had woken her. She usually slept the sleep of the dead, even when under stress—it was almost impossible to wake her in the middle of the night.

Now that she was awake, she felt a little thirsty. She figured she might as well get up for a glass of water. With a yawn, she reached for her glasses, which she never wore except for just before going to sleep and just after waking. Her hand smacked around the surface of her bedside table.

Nothing.

Which wasn't unusual. She was either missing them by a mile, or they'd fallen to the carpeted floor below. With a sleepy groan and a stretch, she reached under the shade of her bedside lamp and turned the switch.

It didn't turn on.

''Odd,'' she muttered to herself. Her subdivision didn't often experience power outages. She groped around for her glasses once more. And then she heard a floorboard creak in the hallway.

''Billy?'' she whispered. But there was no response.

Bending low, she skimmed the carpet with her fingers, hoping to find her glasses. Nothing. She squinted at the entrance to her bedroom, but all she could see was pitch black through the open doorway.

Another creak sounded in the darkness, and an almost painful prickling sensation crept across her skin. Too many coincidences. She whipped one hand behind her, reaching for the familiar Glock she kept in a holster hanging behind her headboard. With a practiced motion, her fingers found the leather strap and moved down to the area where her gun was.

Where her gun should have been.

Empty.

Okay, she'd forgotten to move the Glock from downstairs, she reasoned, even though her heart was hammering in her chest like a piston. Everything was fine, since she kept a single-shot Contender handgun in her top dresser drawer. With her inadequate vision trained on the hopelessly blurred doorway, she catapulted from the bed and across the room. Her body braced against the impact as she hit the dresser, and within seconds, her hand was inside the top drawer, burrowing expertly under the T-shirts she kept there to where the gun should have been. She'd practiced this move so many times, she didn't need to see it to find it.

Gone.

With a whimper, Maggie gripped one of the dresser handles. Her guns. Ignoring the fear that had started creeping up her spine, she lurched across the room back to the dark lump that was the bed, then edged along the mattress until her knee hit the end table once more. She gasped at the sudden pain and reached for the telephone she knew was there. Ignoring her throbbing shin, she put the receiver to her ear.

Dead.

Someone was in her house, he'd disabled her phone, and he had her guns. *There's no time to be scared. Think, Maggie,* she told herself. Grabbing the dark lump she knew was the bedside lamp, she tore off the small shade, then ripped the cord out of the wall. The lamp was metal, and though it wasn't an ideal weapon, it was all she had. She wound the cord around the base so it wouldn't drag.

If she just shut her bedroom door, she could lock herself inside. The door was made of steel, and the locks on it were sound. She could stay in here for days without fear of someone breaching it.

Then she thought of Cartwright and Mason, the two officers guarding her house. Had they heard the intruder? Seen him?

Or maybe he's gotten them, like all good bogeymen do.

But what if he hadn't? What if she locked herself in, and the intruder in her house killed Cartwright and Mason because of it? After all, the Surgeon was adept at sneaking around police. They might still be alive, and they might not even know what had slipped past them in the dark.

Brandishing the lamp in front of her, she tiptoed to the black maw of the open doorway, her stomach clenching at the thought of passing through it. *How can you help them? You can't go outside. You can't even see.*

Ignore it. She had to ignore the voice that taunted her. One blind, agoraphobic ex-cop was better than nothing, if Mason and Cartwright were in danger. Taking a deep breath, Maggie swiveled around so her back was against the wall and edged sideways to the door. She brushed her palm in front of her, waiting until her fingers connected with the raised molding around the doorframe. Dammit, she hadn't even been able to tell by sight what was wall and what was the doorway. Squinting hard, she leaned her head through the opening and checked one side, then the other.

It all looked like one big blur. He could be standing two feet away from her, and she'd never know it because everything around her looked as though it could attack.

Use your other senses. Listen.

Good advice, but all she could hear was the blood rushing in her ears. She crept around the doorjamb and into the hall, feeling like someone trapped in an Impressionist painting done solely in blues and blacks.

One of the shadows dancing around her moved forward. She swung out with the lamp, only to hear a whoosh of air as it connected with nothing. She blinked, and the shadow was gone, if it had even been there in the first place. She felt as if she were moving through water; it was enveloping her, distorting everything around her.

She stepped forward, and the hardwood floor creaked under her feet. Wincing at the sound, she froze, brought the lamp up to protect her face. She took another step. The boards were quiet this time. Inch by agonizing inch, Maggie sidled along the hallway, until she estimated she was mere feet from where it turned sharply to the staircase. Just a few more steps, and she could charge down the stairs and pound on the front door until the officers heard her and came inside.

A brushing sound, like cloth sliding against a wall, caught her attention. Downstairs. The sound came from downstairs.

Oh, God, could she beat him to the door? She tiptoed quickly to where she assumed the corner was, sighing in relief when she felt the break in the wall. She flattened herself against its surface, knowing that anyone downstairs couldn't see her. *What do I do?*

A GOOD SOLDIER knows about timing. An attack had to be exquisitely, perfect sequenced, down to the last millisecond, the last seemingly inconsequential detail. Flawless planning was important. It was what he did best.

He backed into the darkness, melting into the shadows like the invisible man. Like a shadow himself. A bringer of death, a purger of sins.

He watched as the Adversary crept along the halls of her residence. She went beyond the enemy—she was the only one who had ever come close to capturing him. So he called her the Adversary, whenever he was watching her. Tonight, she looked more like one of the enemy soldiers she was always sending against him. She was noisy, and she looked weak. Not at all like the most formidable Adversary he had ever come up against. But perhaps it was all an act, designed to fool him. He was a good soldier—he would not be fooled.

He felt a thrill in his groin at the thought of washing her clean, absolving her of all. *Shameful, sinful son.*

But maybe this time, it wasn't a sin. He admired the Adversary for her worthiness, as the allied armies of Russia, Austria and England might have admired Napoleon at Waterloo. He loved her, in the way that a lion might love the swift, graceful movements of a gazelle.

But the red days were here, and that final battle was almost upon him. And with her death would come everlasting glory.

It was hubris, shameful, sinful hubris to want that glory, but he did want it. He was a good soldier, and good soldiers should be remembered forever.

BEHIND HER, the sanctuary of her bedroom beckoned, but Maggie knew she couldn't give in to the temptation to run back inside it. She had to get to Mason and Cartwright.

Taking a deep breath, she turned the corner and started quietly down the stairs, clutching the lamp to her chest with both hands. She peered down into the hallway through the railing, but everything was blurs and shadows.

Crouching low, Maggie crept along the stairway, knowing that he could jump out of the dark at any moment, and it would all be over. Her hands gripped the lamp until her fingers cramped. It was all she could do to keep putting one foot in front of the other. She heard another brush, and she froze.

The living room. Her eyes went to the entrance of the room right next to her front door, the outline of which was so blurred by her poor vision, she couldn't tell where the walls ended and the room began. If he were in there, he'd catch her before she could get out. And she wouldn't even see him coming.

Better run.

She shot down the rest of the stairs to the door, her body smacking against the slab of wood as she misjudged the distance. Throwing the lamp in the general direction of the living room, she fumbled at the locks with trembling, frantic hands. She heard a footstep, then another, and the sound of low, hideous laughter rang in her ears. No, no, please God, no.

The deadbolt shot back with a snap, and then she was free. She hurled herself onto the porch, squinting in the darkness for some sign of Cartwright and Mason. She called their names.

They didn't answer.

Chapter Ten

"Officer Cartwright?" Maggie hissed in the darkness, closing the door behind her. Nothing. She pressed her lips together, smothering the cry of frustration. He was behind her. And all she had left was the small island of her porch. Go back inside, and he'd kill her for sure. Stay on the porch, and she'd go mad.

Stretching her hands in front of her, Maggie stepped away from the house. Her fingers connected with the support column, and she wrapped her arm around it, standing just above the three stairs, wondering how she'd ever get beyond her front yard. This experiment had gone so well before.

Something smacked against the glass of the living room window behind her, making her jump, making her move. She lurched forward, one hand sweeping blindly in front of her, and her foot connected with the first step.

If you run, he can't get you.

The wind blew the thin cotton pajama pants and T-shirt she was wearing against her body, whipping the material around her legs. She turned her head, trying to make some sense of the shapes around her. The trees should be there, the garage should be there, the ocean should be behind her. But all she could see were blurs and shadows, closing in on her like black fog. The house called to her with a siren's song. Sanctuary.

A wave of dizziness washed over her, giving her the sense that she was in the dark hold of a ship being buffeted by angry water. She swept her hand out in front of her, unseeing. What if she lost consciousness again? What if she went mad?

Another thud sounded behind her, and she screamed, her body lurching blindly forward until she hit the second stair. Oh, God, he was watching her. He was enjoying this.

"Run. You have to run. The outdoors isn't going to kill you, but he will," she told herself, gasping for breath between words. It sounded so reasonable, so sane, but she couldn't make her body obey. She stood, swaying on the second stair, fear and panic crushing her chest, breaking her ribs.

She pressed the heels of her hands against her temples, as if trying to keep her skull from breaking apart.

"Why can't I do this? Why?" she screamed into the inky blackness closing around her. "You deserve to die, you stupid, cowardly woman." Sobbing now, she curled her bare toes into the wooden boards of the stair, getting a pathetic sense of security from the minor contact with some part of her house.

She heard him laugh behind her.

The sound gave her focus. She closed her eyes,

lowered her hands, and oriented herself, balancing her weight evenly on the soles of her feet. Tadasana— mountain pose. She could hear him scratching at the window, ten paces from the door. She was five paces from it. If she ran back inside, she could charge up the stairs, get to her bedroom. Lock herself in. If she went back, she could beat him, and she'd be safe until someone came to find her. Take another step, and she'd go mad.

The things people did to avoid their worst nightmares.

One, she counted mentally. *Two. Three.* Whirling around, Maggie charged back across the porch and hurled her body at the door. It swung open and hit the wall behind it with a bang. She sensed, rather than saw, movement to her left. He was coming for her.

She reached blindly in front of her and connected with the stair railing. Using it for balance, she took the stairs two at a time, propelling herself upward with every ounce of strength she had left.

She stumbled as she hit the top of the landing, her inadequate eyes misjudging the distance. She felt a sharp pain in her ankle as she threw her weight to the right, but she ignored it. Her hand smacked against the wall, and she oriented herself, running blindly toward her bedroom.

She could hear him behind her, coming up the stairs, laughing at her. He didn't know about the steel door.

With one last burst of energy, she hurled herself into the room at the end of the hall and pulled at the door. Feeling as if she were moving in slow motion, she turned, pushed, and watched the door swing shut.

"Get away from me, you son of a bitch," she snarled as the lock clicked into place. And then, through the open window, she heard a car pull into her driveway.

FROM HER POSITION near her back bedroom window, Maggie heard the glass doors at the back of her house whoosh open, and the sound of footsteps running across the brick patio. Then, the intruder stepped onto sand, and she heard nothing else.

Whoever had pulled up had scared him off, obviously. She was safe—for the time being.

Still, leaving her bedroom was more difficult than she would have thought, despite the fact that her tormentor was gone and someone—probably Brentwood—was approaching her front door, and she'd bet he was armed.

Bracing herself, she stepped into the hallway, feeling the first vestiges of panic rising in her throat. At this rate, she'd end up locking herself away in that one room, rather than just the whole house.

As she started down the stairway, she heard the sounds of a key scraping against the lock. The only people to whom she'd given keys were Billy and Adriana. And then someone called out.

She ran the rest of the way down the stairs, her heart in her throat. Billy.

He was here. He was whole.

The door swung open, and Maggie catapulted herself into a Billy-shaped blur. "Don't stay outside," she said breathlessly.

He held her tightly with one arm and allowed her to pull him into the house, the other hand brandishing his gun he'd drawn long before opening the door. The moon broke through the clouds, bathing them both in blue light. She ran her palms along his broad shoulders, not quite able to believe he was really there.

"Why aren't the security lights on?" he asked.

Without letting him go, she told him what had happened, feeling tension move through his frame with every word. "I don't know what happened to Cartwright and Mason. You didn't see them?" she finished.

He pulled out of her arms and shook his head. He looked her up and down clinically, as if to make sure she was really all right. "You were limping," he said. It was a statement, not a question.

"Twisted my ankle. It's nothing," she said. "We need to get Borkowski and Brentwood over here right now. And don't you even think about looking for Cartwright and Mason outside alone."

Pulling a borrowed cell phone from his pocket, he flipped it open and handed it to her. "Borkowski's number five on speed dial. I'm going to get the mag lite out of my laptop case, and then we'll search the house." He kicked the door closed.

Maggie brought the phone close to her nose, skimming her fingers along the out-of-focus buttons to figure out how to activate speed dial.

"Mags?"

''He took my glasses,'' she said, still trying to de-cipher the blurs in front of her. It was funny how little that theft bothered her at that moment, since he was here. She was just so relieved they were both alive. ''My contacts are upstairs.''

Swearing viciously, he took the phone from her and made the call himself. When he was finished, he pocketed the phone and held up his hand. ''How many fingers am I holding up?''

Gripping his wrist, Maggie brought his hand up to her face, until it was almost touching her nose. ''Three.''

''Very funny.'' She heard him shift slightly. ''Your eyesight's that bad without contacts?''

She nodded.

''You must have been terrified,'' he said softly.

Don't think about it. ''I'm fine,'' she replied, a lit-tle more tersely than she'd intended.

The Billy-shaped blob in front of her handed her the flashlight he'd been carrying—one so heavy, it could no doubt double as a weapon. ''Shine this in front of us and hold on to me. We'll search the house to make sure he didn't stay behind, and then we'll get your eyesight back.''

With that he turned, and she put a hand lightly on his broad shoulder, allowing him to guide her through their dark, out-of-focus surroundings. They made a thorough search of every room, and even though she had heard the Surgeon leave through the back patio door, it still made her feel better. Or maybe it was touching Billy, inhaling the clean smell of the soap and shampoo he used, hearing that deep voice of his as it reverberated through to her bones. It was true that when you were deprived of one of your senses, the others compensated, and smell, hearing and touch were working overtime in her case.

When they stepped into the kitchen, Maggie felt a cool wind blow across her body. Even with her poor vision, she could tell that the glass patio doors stood wide open, and she sensed a blur of movement around them—the sheer tab curtains dancing in the nighttime breeze. She swept the flashlight beam across the room, across the counter, the kitchen island, the small table in the breakfast nook, the floor. As she directed the beam toward the entrance to the formal dining room, Billy clamped a hand on her arm.

"Back there," he said. He guided her hand back toward the table, so the flashlight beam illuminated its surface. She stepped closer, the circle of light growing larger, until her upper thighs touched the table's edge. Bending carefully, she lowered her face until her nose nearly touched the surface, so she could see what he'd seen. Though even her up-close vision wasn't great, she could make out the five guns—the same ones that had been hidden throughout her house—lying neatly in a row.

He'd been on every floor, in nearly every room. He knew her house better than anyone else did.

Fixated on the guns, Maggie moved her head so she could closely examine all of them. When she reached the end of the row, she noticed that even her can of Mace and one sharp knife formed part of the macabre still life on the table. Underneath it was another photograph. Without thinking, she reached for it.

Once again, Billy touched her arm, stopping her from leaving her prints on the evidence. She heard him snap on a pair of the ubiquitous FBI-issue latex gloves, then watched as he moved the Mace can and picked up the photo.

"It's out of focus," he said.

She straightened and reached for his arm, pulling herself closer to him so she could see. But he turned away from her and picked something else off the table. With the same gentleness with which he'd put the headset on her earlier that day, he placed her glasses on her face.

Blinking in surprise, Maggie reached for his hand, entwining her fingers in his. With her vision back, she could see he looked pale, the large gauze bandage on his forehead masking what had to be a vicious head wound. "He really hurt you," she said, touching the white gauze with her free hand, the photograph forgotten for the moment. "I thought he'd killed you."

"You and me both, babe." Billy gave her a wry smile. "I didn't even see him coming."

"You wouldn't." The thought made her shudder. She pulled away from him and, with one quick movement, shone the flashlight on the photo Billy held.

It was a picture of him.

She shook her head, wanting desperately to deny what she saw. Most of the photo was blurred, as if someone had smeared oil on the camera lens, but Billy's face was in perfect focus. Feeling suddenly ill, Maggie wrapped her hands around the flashlight and hugged it to her chest, aiming the beam upward so it bounced off the ceiling and bathed the room in a faint glow. "It's you," she said, dazed. "He's coming after you. Because of me."

"Maggie—" He dropped the photo on the table.

"You…" Her voice broke, and she had to swallow her words for a moment to regain her composure. She couldn't cry in front of him. Not now. "You've got to get away from me. I'll get you killed."

Billy put the photo down and tugged off the latex gloves. "That's not true."

"Don't be ridiculous." She made a sound that fell somewhere between a laugh and a sob. She really just felt like screaming. "Of course it's true. He won't stop until I'm dead, and if you stand in his way, you'll die, too."

"I won't," he said. "And neither will you."

"You can't promise me that." Her vision blurred again, and this time, it had nothing to do with her glasses. "No one can."

"I can," he said, and when she looked into his eyes, she almost believed him.

"He'll kill you, and it'll be my fault. Can't you hear what I'm telling you? I've put you in danger."

"No." He took the flashlight away from her and set it on the table, then took her face in his hands and tilted it up toward his. "Maggie, you saved me."

She did laugh at that, through her tears, a scornful, disbelieving sound.

"I was half dead when I met you, and somehow, you made me feel again when I thought I never would." He pressed his lips to her forehead. "I know you're sick, and I know you're afraid, and I know you'd probably rather give up right now rather than wait and see what this monster is going to do to you next. But you are the strongest woman I've ever met in my life, and when I saw you, I knew that if you could live through this and still be whole, I could, too. You saved me, Maggie." He bent his head and brushed his mouth against hers. "I wanted to do nothing but die, and you made me want to live again."

She pulled back and just looked at him, unable to do anything more than blink back tears and process what she'd heard. Saved him? She'd damned near killed him, and he just held her with such gentleness, it nearly ruined her.

She opened her mouth to speak, then closed it when a sob threatened to escape. Who was this man, who could come into her life and make her feel safe enough to walk outside for the first time in almost two years? Who was he, that he could put himself in constant danger for her sake, time and again? He'd accomplished what he'd wanted—the Surgeon's only living victim was part of the task force, wholly dedicated to fleshing out the identity of the murderer. He could have left her at any time, but still he stayed, even though every passing minute made him more visible to a killer's watchful eyes.

"Billy—" she began, reaching for him, wanting something but not stopping to consider what that something was. But then the sound of tires crunching on gravel made her step back, and the spell was broken.

"The police," he said, and he moved away from her to answer the door. Red flashing lights illuminated the yard as Brentwood and Borkowski stepped up to the porch.

"Mason and Cartwright are missing," Billy told them once they had come inside.

Brentwood nodded, twisting a gold ring on the little finger of his left hand. "We found them. They'd parked their car a few blocks down on Asilomar. He'd locked them in the trunk."

"Concussions?" She hoped for the best, since the two detectives didn't look as if they'd just found two of their colleagues murdered.

Borkowski nodded, still in the black suit and beige collared shirt she'd worn to the memorial service. "Knocked them cold. This yard is wide open. I have no idea how he ambushed them like that. It's as if he's invisible. We just loaded them up in an ambulance so they can get checked out, but they'll be okay."

Billy cocked his head toward the kitchen. "I think there's something you need to see."

The four of them went into the kitchen, Brentwood and Borkowski whipping out large, batonlike metal flashlights. The beams from all three did a decent job of lighting up the room. "Pretty guns all in a row," Borkowski said dryly. "I take it these are yours?"

Maggie nodded. "I had them hidden around the house. For protection."

"Some protection." Detective Brentwood shoved his hands in the pockets of his trench coat and rocked back and forth on his heels. "Where were they located?"

"Sugar canister." Maggie pointed at the Firestar that had been inside the blue ceramic container, then indicated each weapon in turn. "Telephone table drawer in the office. Locked in a security box under the living room couch. In a holster hanging on my bed's headboard. In a holster in my top dresser drawer. And that one," she said, gesturing to the yellow spray can of Mace, "was on the table near the front door."

Borkowski did a subtle double take. "He was in your bedroom?"

Somehow, hearing the words spoken aloud brought back the almost paralyzing fear. "He must have been. No one else moved these guns. And my glasses."

Brentwood stopped rocking for a moment. "He's watching you. And often, if he knows where the things you keep hidden inside your house are."

Maggie shuddered, not wanting to think about her torturer standing at her windows, observing her with only a pane of thin glass between them. But she had to—James was right. There was not other way he could have broken in and gone right for her weapon stash with such expediency. "It fits his behavior patterns. He watches through windows, follows your every move. He's looking for the perfect time and place to jump out of the shadows and get you. And you won't even see him coming.''

Borkowski made a face. "Excuse me. I think my skin just crawled into the next room.'' The tough detective's words displayed a surprising vulnerability, Maggie thought, coming from a female cop who'd probably had to work twice as hard as a man to get where she was. Obviously, the case was getting to all of them.

Not that many people wouldn't be deeply troubled by an invisible sociopath who disarmed seasoned police officers and made women disappear with ease.

''Why do you think he didn't kill Mason and Cartwright, or Hayes and Lockwood earlier, for that matter?'' Brentwood asked.

Maggie shrugged. ''Who really knows? The Son of Sam heard voices coming from his neighbor's dog, telling him who to kill. My best guess is that something inside him lets him know who his next victim should be. Everyone else is just an obstacle to that goal. Or it could be his way of thumbing his nose at the police. They're not important enough to kill,'' she added.

''Tell us what happened tonight,'' Brentwood interjected.

Maggie explained in detail the twisted cat-and-mouse game she and the intruder had played, and then Billy produced the photo—which he'd bagged in plastic—that the Surgeon had left behind. Once again,

Maggie was almost overcome at the way Billy's face stood out among the blurred shapes around him in an obvious message.

"The twelfth victim," Brentwood murmured, referring to the extra number on the Surgeon's earlier note, where he'd given himself twelve kills instead of his actual eleven. "Do you think he's trying to tell us it's going to be you?"

Billy shrugged, not looking terribly concerned about the possibility of being targeted by a serial killer. "I think it's misdirection. Maggie says he only gets off on killing women."

"Be that as it may, he's definitely making a threat here." Borkowski turned to Maggie. "Would he kill a man? Could he deviate that much from his standard M.O.?"

Now it was Maggie's turn to shrug. "He could," she began tentatively, running through the different possibilities in her mind. "The Zodiac killer murdered both men and women in ways that broke every rule about how his type of killer was supposed to act. But I think Billy's right. The Surgeon wouldn't get the same enjoyment out of going after a man. He might be making this threat to terrorize me."

"Charming," Borkowski muttered under her breath. "I think it's safe to assume he could come after either one of you at any moment. From now on, we're putting officers at your doors and on both ends of your street twenty-four/seven. Billy, he took your cell phone earlier today, right?"

Billy nodded.

"Maybe he's trying to establish a line of communication. I'll call the number from the station and let him know we're listening." She turned to Maggie. "If you hear, see or just get the slightest sense that something's wrong, you let the officers outside your house know, got it?"

"Got it," Maggie replied.

"And you—" She pointed at Billy. "I know how well you respond to orders, but I strongly advise you not to go anywhere without another person, preferably someone with a badge and a gun."

Billy just raised an eyebrow at her.

"Call me, Billy, anytime," Borkowski said, her tone that of a pleading friend instead of a police detective. "And both of you," she added, "watch your backs."

Chapter Eleven

When Brentwood and Borkowski finally left, it was almost dawn, and Billy felt an exhausted coldness seep through his bones. After turning the power back on, Billy moved quickly through the rooms and hallways, checking the locks on every last door and window.

They'd come so close to losing Maggie tonight, and the thought made him want to head outside and hunt the Surgeon down until he found him. But at this point, he didn't dare leave Maggie alone. The killer was obviously getting closer to making a move against her—his appearance at Gina's memorial service had been a deadly misdirection aimed at keeping police focus away from Maggie herself.

And they'd all fallen for it—the same way Billy had fallen for the fallacy that work was more important than his only remaining family member many months ago.

He stumbled through the hallway, trying unsuccessfully to block out the memories, and then his elbow accidentally connected with a hall cabinet in a blow that reverberated throughout the house. He hissed with pain and backed away, into Maggie's office. A sharp pain burned through his entire arm.

Good, he thought, wiping his throbbing hand against the rough fabric of his jeans. It gave him something else to concentrate on besides the cold.

Moving toward one of the large windows on the far wall of the room, he watched the sky turn from indigo to red-violet as the first rays of the morning sun flowed across the ocean like liquid. How many mornings had he watched, wondering why the sun kept coming up when Jenna was dead, why he continued to breathe and eat and live when he'd as good as killed his sister. He braced his arm against the window frame and leaned his forehead on it, his breath coming in ragged gasps as he watched that damn sun come up one more time.

As light slowly grew brighter, the pain in his hand subsided, and his breathing regulated again. All of it felt like a small betrayal. Reaching into his back pocket, he took out his wallet and removed a photo with one ragged edge from one of the clear, plastic sleeves inside. He touched the surface of the picture, feeling the familiar hollowness in his chest as he cupped it in his hand.

"What are you doing awake?" he asked hoarsely without turning around.

"I came to ask you the same question," Maggie responded behind him. He turned to watch her pad into the room behind him, her pajama pants slung low on her hips. She tugged the hem of her short gray

T-shirt down over the edge of her waistband as she came to stand next to him. "It's so beautiful out there," she said wistfully, staring out at the rainbow-hued water. Her arm brushed his with a featherlight softness.

His hand closed over the picture he held, but not before she noticed. "Nice picture," she said. "You look happy."

"I was," he said.

She reached over and uncurled his fingers from the photo. "The hand on your shoulder—Jenna used to be in this?" she asked, pointing to the empty space to the right of the torn edge.

He nodded, feeling his throat close off again. And then Maggie moved behind him. Her arms wrapped around his waist, and her cheek rested in the hollow between his shoulder blades.

"I'm sorry, Billy," she said. "It wasn't your fault. There's nothing else I can say, because you have to come to that conclusion on your own. But I know, I *know* it wasn't your fault."

They remained like that, silent, her arms holding him together, until his spirit grew quiet. The torn photo fell out of his fingers to the floor. He didn't want to be quiet.

"Let go of me, Mags," he said. "You don't want to be here right now."

She tightened her grip. "I do," she said.

"I can't—" He stopped, afraid she'd hear something in his voice that he didn't want to reveal. "I can't do this. I have to— Jenna is all that matters right now.''

He expected her to remind him that Jenna was dead, but all she said was, ''I know.'' Then he felt her lips move against his shirt, transferring their warmth to the skin of his back. ''Maybe I'm not asking for 'this.' Maybe I'm just asking for one night.'' Her hands slipped away from his waist, and then she ran her palms up his back in a slow, languid movement that nearly drove him mad with wanting her. ''Maybe we both need it.''

He turned around in her arms. ''You don't know what you're asking,'' he said. God help him, he was shaking.

''You're wrong,'' she whispered, her dark, gypsy eyes on fire. For him.

''Get out of here,'' he said hoarsely. He put his hands on her shoulders as if to push her away, but then he found himself gripping the thin cotton of her T-shirt and pulling her closer, until their lips were almost touching. ''Get out of my head,'' he whispered against her mouth.

She reached up to cup his face in her small hands, then kissed him with a sweet softness that was as intoxicating as wine. With more control than he thought he possessed, he brushed his lips against her forehead, her temple, the bone of her cheek, the corner of her full, beautiful mouth, and he felt her relax into the arms he hadn't even realized he'd wrapped around her. ''Maggie,'' he murmured. ''What are you doing to me?''

"Just loving you, Billy," she said.

A sound between a groan and a cry escaped him then, and he brought his mouth to hers, as desire ripped through his body. She kissed him back with a fury and passion that shouldn't have surprised him, but it did anyway. Her hands ran through his hair, and her body moved into his as if she'd go right through him.

He felt something tugging on the buttons of his shirt, and then, before he had a chance to think about whether this was a wise idea, he was slipping out of it. A few seconds later, he felt the material bunched up in the small of his back, held there by one of her hands as the other roamed across his bare skin. He reached behind him and tugged the shirt out of her fingers, backing away from her.

"I don't belong in your neat little world, Mags." He threw the shirt to the ground.

Her eyes flicked briefly to the side, and then she stared up at him, her face unreadable. "It doesn't matter."

"So in control," he murmured. He backed away from her and swept a hand along one of her bookshelves, sending several of her thick hardcovers tumbling to the floor. But she didn't reach for the scattered items on the ground—she reached for him. He fell into her arms and tangled his fingers in her thick, beautiful hair, tied up in that damned ponytail. She gasped. "I want to make you lose it," he said.

He cupped her behind with one hand and lifted her until her legs were wrapped around his hips, and the way she moved against him made his vision blur. He stumbled toward the desk and swept an arm across it, sending the neat stack of files and their contents flying. Papers and photographs rained down on the floor, leaving the surface smooth and bare, and he lowered her down on it. "Don't even think about looking at the floor, Mags," he murmured in her ear, then bit softly down on her earlobe.

"What floor?" she murmured. He laughed softly, then dragged his mouth down her neck. She arched her back as he hit a sensitive spot, and the soft noises she made nearly blew the top off his head.

Then he felt her slide underneath him, her hips doing incredible things to his body. Her feet connected with the floor, and she shoved him off her with one solid push. He started to back away, thinking she was telling him to stop, praying that she wasn't.

"Maybe I like control," she said, pressing against his shoulder until he stepped backward. Blindly, he reached for her and pulled her roughly toward him. They ended up on the window seat, with his back against the glass and her straddling his hips. Their mouths came together with such force that he thought they might break the glass and go spilling out on the sand, washing away on the ocean. He pulled on the clip that held her hair, and it came cascading around them like a black waterfall.

He moved his hands over her full breasts, along the insides of her thighs. She closed her eyes, and a soft "ohhh" escaped her. "Maybe I like it more," he said. And then her hand moved between them, brushing against the fly of his jeans, and all coherent thoughts left him.

With a groan, he slipped his own hand under the hem of her T-shirt, his fingers nearly spanning her waist as he touched the bare skin of her back. It felt like velvet. "Are you sure you want this, Mags?" he ground out, the hazy part of his mind that still worked bracing itself for her answer.

She pulled back and looked at him with her wild eyes, a small, private smile tipping up the corners of her mouth. Then, she lifted her body off his and stood. He took a deep, shuddering breath and raised himself up on his elbows, aching for her, forcing himself not to lunge forward and take her on the floor, right then and there.

She gripped the waistband of her pants and pulled. All he could do was watch while the fabric skimmed her lithe, incredible legs until it puddled around her ankles, and she was standing before him in a T-shirt and little else.

He wasn't quite sure what happened next, but lunging was definitely involved. The next thing he knew, the two of them were on the soft wool carpet, caught in a tangle of bodies that felt so damn good. He shifted so she was lying on her back and he was on top of her, her head cradled between his forearms. He reached out and let a stray curl slip like silk between his fingers. "Your hair," he whispered, "is the most erotic thing I've ever seen."

She raised her head and kissed him with a passion that bordered on madness. "Billy," she murmured as he moved his mouth down the side of her neck, to her collarbone, down farther still to the hollow between her breasts, just above the neckline of her shirt. "Billy," she said again, "shouldn't we be on a bed?"

He was just about to answer her when her hands went to his waistband. She undid the top button of his fly and started working on the zipper, her fingers brushing against him in places and ways that drove him crazy with wanting her. "To hell with the bed," he gasped.

Her musical laughter sounded in his ear, but then he slipped his hands underneath her shirt, and her laughter turned to something more heated. He tugged the shirt upward.

She clamped both hands on his wrist.

He froze. "What is it?"

Her expression had gone from one of intense desire to one of aching vulnerability. "I just...I have..." Her voice wavered. "Oh, God, they're so..."

Billy shifted until he was leaning on his side, resting his upper body on one of his elbows. He placed a hand against her flat abdomen, feeling slight ridges under the cotton of her shirt. Once again, she snapped a hand around his wrist. He tugged his hand upward and turned his wrist so his palm was cupping hers. Then, he lifted her hand to his lips. "I know what you have, Mags," he said, his eyes locking with hers. "You don't have to hide them. Not from me."

Her breath caught, and she could only stare at him as the seconds ticked by. With agonizing slowness, she pulled her hand out of his, and he held perfectly still, waiting, wanting her to make the first move. Wanting her.

She gripped the hem of her shirt, twisting the material between her fingers.

He waited.

Finally, closing her eyes tightly as if she were bracing herself to swan dive off a cliff, she pulled the shirt over her head. She wasn't wearing a bra underneath. She was perfect.

The first rays of sunlight streamed through the glass panes of the window, and the angry scars on her stomach glowed golden. She covered them with the flat of her hand, her eyes still closed.

He reached out and touched her, butterfly soft touches on her collarbone, around the curve of one perfect breast, then traced one of the scars her hand couldn't cover.

"You're so beautiful," he said. And she was.

Her dark eyes opened, and she reached up to touch his cheek. "So are you," she said.

He needed to get her to a bed, he thought, before he was so far gone, he'd take her right then and there on the carpet. He rose, reaching a hand down to help her stand. Then, he picked her up, cradled her in his arms and carried her from the office to her bedroom upstairs.

IT WASN'T UNTIL early the next afternoon that Billy finally fell asleep, with one arm thrown over his head and the other resting on her thigh. Not doing anything, just resting—and making it very difficult for her to get up without waking him. But she had to get up. She had to leave.

Inhaling slowly through her teeth, she slid carefully across the bed. She disengaged herself from Billy's hand as smoothly as she could, kicking away the sheets that confined her with slow, deliberate movements. And, just when she thought she was home free, she made the mistake of looking at him.

Some people toss and turn in their sleep, others talk, and still others flinch and make faces. Not Billy. He seemed to completely relax while sleeping—his hair falling over his smooth forehead, his dark eyelashes resting gently on his cheeks. The sheets where bunched around his lean waist, and his body was sprawled over every available inch of his half of the bed. He looked younger. He looked free.

He also snored like a big dog. It was sort of endearing.

She indulged herself for a moment and just watched him, and the watching made her want him all over again. He looked peaceful when he slept. Maggie wished he could look like that just once while awake. Just once.

But he never would—at least not while he knew her. They'd work together, and maybe they'd even bring down the Surgeon. Maybe that would make Maggie better, but what then? She'd be a constant reminder of all he'd lost, she and the ugly scars on her stomach that matched the postmortem cuts on his sister's body.

How could he possibly want her after this was all over?

She pushed off the bed and bolted for the door. Behind her, Billy stirred on the bed, but she didn't wait to see if he'd wake up completely. She didn't think she could stay in that room with Billy for one more minute. Not without losing it completely. She'd wanted this so much last night. She still wanted him now.

Grabbing a quilt that had ended up on the floor sometime during the morning, she headed for the stairs, pulling it around her as she walked. In a matter of seconds, she was in her office, the door locked behind her. The normally gorgeous view from the window seat was obscured by the thickest fog she had ever seen, and it gave the impression that the house was floating in a cloud.

She folded herself onto the seat and stared out into the mist, catching only the most occasional glimpses of Asilomar Beach. Gripping the edges of the quilt at her collarbone, she tugged the material tighter around herself, wondering if she'd ever be warm enough again.

Billy was such a wonderful person, in so many ways. When losing his entire family the way he had would have wrecked most people, he remained strong in all the ways that counted. He joked with her when she needed it, held her when she cried. He didn't make her feel like a freak when the mere sight of her front yard made her pass out in fear.

He'd thrown himself in front of a rookie cop, taking a blow that could have killed him.

He'd held Kelli Ransom's hand for hours after her friend's horrible death, comforting her until her family arrived when most people would have walked away.

God, he'd even played chess with her.

And here she was, getting ready to kill whatever it was between them before it had a chance to get started, before she could even find out how Billy felt about the matter.

It's better this way, she thought. *It'll hurt less now than later.*

She was sick, he was in pain, all because of the same twisted man. They'd never heal as long as they were together. They'd always remember. And the remembering would drive them mad.

Comfort, she told herself. They'd comforted each other when no one else could have possibly understood what they were going through. That's all she'd wanted. That's all it was. She wrapped the quilt tighter around her shoulders and watched the fog swirl around her house.

Then why did it feel like so much more?

WHEN BILLY OPENED his eyes, the first thing he saw was Maggie tearing out of the bedroom like she'd just slept with Chewbacca. Way to put her at ease, champ. After four hours of the most wildly passionate sex he'd ever had, he'd simply rolled over and fallen asleep, leaving her to think about whatever it was that women thought about the morning after.

Not exactly what Casanova would have done, was it?

Maybe he should find her and tell her. He felt incredible. He'd just enjoyed the first real, honest-to-goodness sleep he'd had in months. He still wanted her.

He was falling in love with her.

Whoa.

Mad, passionate sex was one thing, but love? He'd been driven by vengeance for so long, he wondered how there could be room for any other emotion. But there it was.

Love wasn't exactly convenient right now. It definitely wasn't kosher, given that he was supposed to protect her. Love was a distraction—and distractions could be deadly.

Love hurt like a bitch when you lost it.

He sat up, leaning his back against the headboard, and scrubbed a hand across his face. Maybe he was just tired.

Right.

In one furious motion, he threw off the covers and got out of bed, scowling. Maybe a shower would help.

A few minutes later, he realized that it hadn't. He needed to talk to Maggie. Dressed in jeans and a navy blue Angels T-shirt, he went downstairs, and was surprised to discover her standing in her front doorway. She'd obviously showered in the first-floor bathroom—her hair hung in damp ringlets down her back.

And, unfortunately, she was wearing clothes—a pair of jeans and a dark-red sweater that hung loosely at her waistband.

He made a point of thumping loudly down the stairs, so he wouldn't startle her. "What are you doing, Mags?" he asked. He ached to touch her, but he refrained.

"You'd think it would be easy," she said. "If I just willed it strongly enough, I could do it." Her dark-brown eyes were focused on the sand-dusted brick walkway that led from the driveway to her house. "It should be that simple."

He did touch her then, placing his hands on her shoulders, letting her know he was there, that she could lean back against him if she wanted. "It's never that simple, Mags," he said.

She sighed. "Sometimes, I just don't understand. Why can't I do it? Why does the world start to spin? Why am I threatened by trees? Trees?" She threw her palms up, then let her arms drop to her sides again. "Ridiculous, really. But I know that if I tried to go get my mail, it would be the hardest thing in the world."

He squeezed her shoulders. "A lot of people would be worse off after what happened to you," he said.

"Sure, and a lot of people would be able to walk outside and get over it." She turned to face him. "Billy, why are you here?"

"What do you mean?"

"You could be part of the task force without camping out here," she said. "But you stay, even though it puts you in danger. The Surgeon doesn't enjoy killing men, but he will. If they get in his way.'' Her hair was back up in that damned ponytail, and she smoothed the sides with both hands. It looked like a nervous habit. ''You've done what you've set out to do—you got the Surgeon's only living victim to be part of the case. Why do you stay?''

''You need someone here—'' he began.

''The police could protect me as well as you can,'' she interrupted. ''I've been thinking about what you said once, that this is a bad idea.''

''What 'this?''' he asked.

She twirled a hand at the wrist, searching for the right words. ''We're in pain, and we feel vulnerable right now. Of course we'd be drawn to each other, but—''

He gently tugged her forward and closed the door behind them, letting his hands fall to his sides after they were inside. ''When I first came here, my goal was simple—I wanted to find the man who'd killed my sister,'' he said, an emotion he couldn't name welling up inside him. Maybe he was saying too much, but at the moment, he didn't care. ''But then things got complicated. You didn't look at me with pity. You didn't tell me to get over it. You were just there, smiling at me, touching me, making me feel—'' he stopped, jamming his hands through his hair ''—something. For the first time since I lost Jenna, I could feel something else, see something else other than those goddamned crime scene photos when I closed my eyes at night.'' He stepped into her space, so he had to look down to see her face, and traced her hairline with his fingers. "You're in my heart. You took away the nightmares."

MAGGIE GASPED and closed her eyes, but not before the tears spilled out of them. His words made her ache—so much. "Billy, you deserve better."

"Mags—"

"You know, I love it when you call me that." The corners of her mouth tilted upward in a sad smile. "Honestly, I don't know what you were going to say after that truly lovely speech. Maybe you were about to tell me we just made the biggest mistake of your life. In which case, I'm going to feel like a giant moron."

"I'd never tell you that," he said.

"No, you wouldn't." She couldn't back away, not while he was still touching her, so she looked down at the floor. "No matter what."

He tipped her chin upward and brushed his lips against hers in the softest of touches. It still set her on fire. "I'd never say that, because I don't feel it," he said.

She blinked rapidly for a few seconds and pulled out of his arms. The distance between them felt like miles. "I feel it," she said.

He grew quiet. She turned away. She'd never expected three words to hurt so much.

"I made a mistake, Billy."

His hand reached up to toy with the spire-shaped

finial on the stairway newel post, his face completely devoid of expression.

"I need to get better, you need to heal." She folded her arms, trying desperately not to reach for him. "How can you move on with someone like me? I'm not normal. And you'll never be normal as long as you're with me."

"Maybe you shouldn't be telling me what I need," he said.

"I don't—" She stopped, unable to give voice to the lie. "I made a mistake. It can't happen again."

He didn't say anything, but fastened those mysterious gray eyes on her and shook his head. Murmuring something that sounded like, "Ah, Mags," he turned away from her and left the room. She heard him pick up a set of keys in the kitchen, and then he headed toward the front door.

"Where are you going?" she asked, then immediately regretted it. Sure, tell the guy to leave in so many words, and then sound all broken-hearted when he did what you asked.

"Out," he replied. "I'll tell the cops down the street to come in closer to the house."

She watched him shrug into his black leather jacket. Then, before she could stop herself, she blurted, "You didn't want to say anything? I mean, I just want to make sure everything's okay between us, and I sort of rambled there for awhile...." She trailed off, feeling stupid and very, very empty.

"Everything's fine," he said, his voice a low rumble. "And you pretty much said it all, didn't you?"

BY THE TIME it was dark, Billy still hadn't returned. And Maggie had to admit, she was hating every minute that he was gone. Sure, there were two police officers on her porch and squad cars parked at each entrance to her road, but she missed him. She turned away from the living room window, with its view of the empty driveway, and headed for the kitchen to make a pot of coffee.

It was better this way. She knew it was, and yet part of her wondered if the ache in her chest would ever go away.

As she was pouring a small amount of coffee beans into her grinder, the beans pinging against the appliance's metal sides, the phone rang. She ignored it.

But then she thought it might be Billy.

Maggie dropped the bag of beans on the counter and lunged for the phone. "Hello?" she said, a little breathlessly, into the receiver.

"Hello, Maggie," a tinny voice replied. "We haven't talked in a while."

Him.

Maggie felt her skin prickle, and a wave of mild nausea rocked her insides. "Who is this?"

"You know who this is." He'd distorted his voice with an electronic voice disguiser. It might have been some kids who'd seen the *Scream* movies one too many times playing a prank, but she knew better. She knew that voice, down in the most secret places of her heart she knew that voice.

"What do you want, then?" she asked with a bravado she wasn't even close to feeling.

"I don't think red is your color. I prefer you in blue."

Maggie looked down at the red cropped sweater she was wearing, remembered the navy blue suit she'd had on when he'd kidnapped her in New Orleans.

"You can see me," she said, taking care to keep her voice neutral. She walked to the window, standing so close, her breath made a circle on the glass, and scanned the beach outside. The fog had burned off during the day, and though the sun was setting, she could still see several people walking along the sand far to the left of her house. Maybe one of them was him. Maybe he was closer than that. "Where are you?"

"Tsk, tsk," he said. "What fun would that be?"

"Oh, I don't know." She pulled the blinds shut with a snap. "Throw me a bone here. I know how you like a challenge."

"Did you enjoy my visit?"

She heard the sound of gravel crunching outside under car tires, and her head snapped around. "It was lovely," she said dryly, her tone belying the fact that she had to grip the phone extra-hard to keep it from falling out of her shaking hands. "Just don't do it again."

"Oh, I'll do it again. We have some unfinished business, you and I," he said.

Heading for the door, she fought to control her speeding pulse and trembling body. "Yeah? So you came into my house while I was sleeping. Big deal.

You had to drug me in New Orleans to take me down. And I'm going to make it a heck of a lot harder on you the second time around.''

"Shut up, bitch!" he shouted, the voice disguiser doing nothing to hide the fact that the caller was very close to losing control. "I'm going to make you beg me to kill you while I cut you open, and then I'll leave your head on a pike for your boyfriend to find."

Billy. Stifling the scream that was welling up in her throat, she nearly leapt to the door to peer through the peephole at the front yard. The two cops were still on her porch, and Billy's car was in the driveway. She saw him heading up the walk, and she pulled open the door to intercept him.

Her sudden presence made him stop in his tracks. She motioned him inside with a frantic wave of her hands. "So why did you take that policeman's cell phone?" Maggie asked into the phone. It was both a question and a way to let Billy know what was going on.

Billy murmured something to the two cops and followed her to the kitchen.

"You mean Special Agent William Corrigan of the FBI?" the caller asked.

Her stomach clenched.

"I guess," she said, her voice noncommittal, even bored-sounding.

"All the better to call you with, my dear," he said.

Of course. They couldn't trace the phone's owner, since that person was Billy. She glanced up at Billy to tell him that the killer was using Billy's phone, but he'd disappeared into the office.

"Why the photo?" she asked.

"Figure it out. I'll give you three guesses."

She headed into the office, where Billy was, to her surprise, typing furiously on his laptop. "Agent Corrigan is your next victim?" she asked.

"Hmmm," the caller said. "Interesting."

A map of the San Francisco Bay area blinked onto the computer screen, and a red circle danced across the area, highlighting Carmel, Pacific Grove, Monterey.

"Okay, you just want me to think Agent Corrigan is your next victim, but it's really me." Maggie bent at the waist to better peer over Billy's shoulder. She covered the phone's mouthpiece with one hand so the caller wouldn't hear the rapid rat-a-tat-tat of Billy's fingers hitting the keys.

"Also intriguing. Try again," the voice said. The caller was calmer now, enjoying being the one in control.

The red circle on the computer screen had settled over Monterey, and then the map zoomed in, revealing the names of city streets and landmarks.

Maggie walked to her desk and studied a copy of the photo the Surgeon had left in her house. Billy's face was in sharp relief, though she noticed that there were two figures standing behind him in the blurred portion of the photo. "You're going after someone else entirely."

"Not specific enough, Maggie," the caller said.

"Okay, you're—"

"Three strikes, and you're out!" the metallic voice shouted over her. "Tell Agent Corrigan freaking won't find me."

"Wait—" she said. His statement made no sense.

Billy stopped his lightning assault on the keyboard for a split second and punched the computer's return button. The map zoomed in again, so the red circle covered an area just south of the U.S. Naval Reserve and northeast of Mermaid Point.

The phone went dead.

"Damn!" Billy slammed a fist onto the desk.

She stared at the red circle. He'd traced the Surgeon's call. She didn't know how he'd done it, but he'd done it. The area inside the red circle on the map covered at least ten city blocks, but it was a start. A big start.

He scrubbed a hand down his face. "I almost had him."

"He said to tell you that you freaking won't find him, or something like that," she said.

Billy's head snapped up.

"His exact words were, 'Tell Agent Corrigan that freaking won't find me,'" she explained, hoping he could make sense out of the Surgeon's cryptic comment.

Billy sat back and swiveled around in the desk chair so his entire body faced her. "It's *phreaking,* with a *ph,*" he said. "It means hacking the phone system. People usually do it to get free long distance or eavesdrop on conversations. It's a first step into hacking.''

''So he's challenging you on your home territory,'' she said. ''Unbelievable.''

An unholy gleam lit up Billy's gray eyes. ''Not to mention stupid,'' he said. ''But it fits. First the bots to find you, and now this. Has he ever done this kind of thing before, to your knowledge?''

She shook her head. ''No, but we still don't know that much about how he chose his victims.''

''Maybe he's a beginner, and maybe he's not'' Billy said. ''But if he wants to play on my home turf, that means I can find him.''

AFTER THEY'D BRIEFED Brentwood and Borkowski on what had just taken place, Billy explained the program he'd used to track the phone. Knowing that the Surgeon had taken his phone, he said, he'd figured the killer would use it to harass Maggie. Some time ago, Billy had programmed the phone's unique Electronic Serial Number and transmission frequency into his laptop, then created a program designed to pinpoint the location of anyone making calls from that phone.

''Cellular phone transmissions travel via cellular towers. The geographical area each tower covers is called a cell, and all of these are connected to the main cellular network,'' he explained. ''Using the ESN imprint, the program on my laptop queries the main cellular network as to which cells my phone is transmitting from. Most programs like it can only pinpoint the cell, but this one can zero in on the caller within a city block—as long as he keeps a connection going.''

Maggie blinked at him. ''I have no idea what you just said, but I'm getting somewhat turned on.''

Billy laughed, and again, Maggie was struck by how unfamiliar the sound was. ''Basically, it's a fast way to trace calls made from my cell phone.''

''And you made this program because...?'' She twirled her hand at the wrist, gesturing for Billy to fill in the rest of the sentence.

He scratched the dark stubble on his cheeks with one hand and looked thoughtful. ''Had a theory. Wanted to see if it worked.'' Then he leaned in closer to examine the computer screen. ''Wait. What's this?''

Maggie followed his finger to an area of green space caught in the red circle's outline. ''It's Iris Canyon Park. A mostly wooded area, with running paths and some big trees,'' she said.

''Big and secluded, like the swamps back home?'' he asked.

Of course.

Just then, Borkowski stepped into the office, knocking on the doorframe as she walked inside. ''I have something to show you,'' she said.

The detective dropped her briefcase on the desk and snapped it open, then pulled out a copy of the front and back of one of the photographs the Surgeon had left behind.

''Agfa paper,'' she explained. ''Most photo developers around here use Kodak, so we went to every one in the general area and asked what kind of paper they used for their photographs.''

''That's brilliant,'' Maggie said. ''So what was the result?''

''Only two independents used Agfa, but every CVC drugstore in the area develops their prints on it. That leaves us with 12 in the area, five of which are somewhat near this house,'' Borkowski said. ''Not sure how helpful that is at this point, but maybe in the future.''

''Are any of those stores inside this circle?'' Billy cocked his head at the map on his computer screen.

Borkowski leaned down and squinted at it, reaching up to brush a stray brown curl out of her face. ''Yeah. There's one on Aguajito Street, just outside the park.... That's just inside the area your program traced his call from, isn't it?'' she asked. Billy nodded.

Borkowski scribbled notes furiously into her small notebook, her pen making rapid scratching sounds against the cheap paper. Then she stopped and flattened her mouth, tapping her pen to her pale, freckled cheek. ''I doubt if he was expecting us to trace the photographs, but this 'phreaking' thing sounds like an outright challenge,'' she said. ''Maybe there's something there he wants us to find.''

The three of them grew quiet, all of them thinking about what that something might be—a missing person turned victim, another photograph or the killer himself.

''All right then,'' Borkowski said suddenly, her voice matter-of-fact. ''Let's get it done.''

Chapter Twelve

Once again, Maggie found herself at the window, watching Billy and the two detectives preparing to canvas the park and surrounding area while she stayed behind. They'd narrowed the Surgeon's location down to a small area of the city, and now, to one small park. Obviously, the Surgeon was getting restless, and it was making him sloppy. Either that, or he was waiting for them, like a giant spider about to ambush an unsuspecting fly.

She shook herself, clearing the negative thoughts from her head. *He's just a man.* One man who, sooner or later, was bound to make a mistake.

And now he'd made two. Using Agfa paper and stealing Billy's phone.

The thought should have left her elated, but she couldn't escape the nagging feeling tugging at her like a belligerent child. *What if it's a trap?*

She heard the front door's hinges squeal in protest as the door opened, and then Billy stepped inside, to her surprise. She heard the sound of Borkowski and

Brentwood's car revving up and then driving off. "You're not going with them?" she asked.

He shook his head. "I'm not leaving you."

"Oh," she said. *Thank God.*

"And, I've got an idea. Mind if I use your office?"

"Of course not."

With that, he disappeared into the other half of the house, and she moved into the living room and plunked down on the sofa with a sigh. Things had been somewhat strained between them since... Maggie didn't even want to think about what came after that *since,* but she couldn't help the hitch in her pulse that accompanied the merest scrap of memory about That Night.

Damn.

Reaching for the stack of folders she'd brought out earlier from the office, Maggie spread out the copies of the files from the Markson and Rhodes murders on the coffee table. She added the copy of the photo of Billy to the papers on the table and scrutinized it closely. The background was blurred, but she knew that there were two people standing behind him, one in white, the other in brown. The one in white was mostly cut out of the picture. The other was standing next to Billy, with his or her entire body, including the face, completely out of focus.

What was she missing?

WITH LIGHTNING SPEED, Billy typed an Internet address into the Web browser on his laptop. He hit Enter with a hard smack, and, suddenly, the screen went black. He waited patiently until a small green cursor appeared at the top of the screen. To most people, it would have looked as if Windows had shut down and the computer was in some variation of DOS mode. Billy knew better.

"Hello," he typed.

The cursor blinked at him.

He waited.

Finally, eight letters appeared one by one, in painstakingly slow fashion, underneath his greeting. "Password?" they read.

Anyone watching would have wondered at the impossible chain of letters and symbols Billy entered, completely from memory. After he'd typed in exactly 26 characters, the screen went black once more, and then he was in.

The screen looked like any other chat room, black letters on an uninventive white background, with the sentence *Welcome to the Network* emblazoned on the top. Below, two people named CyberPhreak and Chemical X were conversing via their PCs about the merits of Linux versus Unix—a novice topic if he ever saw one.

He pounded on the keyboard, and a tenth of a second later, his words appeared on the white screen.

TheGuardian: Where's the Room?
CyberPhreak: What room? You're in it, dude.

The Network was one of the best-known hacker hangouts on the Internet, and it was without fail the first place wannabe hackers and those who were merely curious came to find out the secrets of the Internet. However, what most people didn't know was that the Network's main Internet address wasn't really the Network. The actual chatroom changed daily, and it was only open to those who knew enough to ask— and who could get through the Gatekeepers. Today, CyberPhreak and Chemical X apparently were charged with that task, and Cyber looked like s/he might be stubborn about giving out the Network's location. He tried again.

TheGuardian: Where's the Room?
Chemical X: Dude! Don't you know who this is, Cyber?
CyberPhreak: No. Should I?
Chemical X: I'll give you a hint.... Only the greatest hacker who ever lived, you moron! Who hasn't heard of TheGuardian? Busted into the Pentagon in less than an hour on his first try. Shut down the European Stock Exchange for an entire day. Invented Interceptor. He's a legend, man.

Billy grimaced. Although he'd used his old screen name to get access, his teenage pranks weren't exactly the kinds of things he wanted to be known for.

CyberPhreak: Billy Phreakin' Corrigan? No way!
Chemical X: Way!
CyberPhreak: NO WAY!

Chemical X: STOP SHOUTING!
CyberPhreak: I heard he went all white hat, dude. Secret agent or something. He's probably here to bust you for that Kentucky thing you pulled last week.
Chemical X: Shut up, man.

And this was getting him absolutely nowhere. Figuring that the one who'd heard of him would be most helpful, he queried Chemical X on ICQ—an instant messenger program—for a private conversation.

TheGuardian: Hey, X, I need to know where the Room is.
Chemical X: Are you here to bust someone, dude, because I could lose my access if I talk to you.
TheGuardian: I just want to talk.
Chemical X: No, the Phreak is right. I heard you're working for the pheds.

Billy rolled his eyes. The Pheds. Why he had ever thought replacing every *F* in the English language with a *ph* was cool was beyond him. But he had to tread carefully here. If he couldn't gain Chemical X's confidence, he'd never find the Network—and his one potential lead on the Surgeon would be that much more difficult to pursue. He decided to try the truth.

TheGuardian: I work for the FBI. We're trying to find a guy who's killed at least 11 women across the country.

Chemical X: Whoa. I'm sorry, dude. Here's the URL....

A numeric Internet address flashed across the ICQ screen.

Chemical X: I'm on break from school, so I've been the Network Gatekeeper a lot. Can I help?
TheGuardian: Seen any newbies around looking for info on phreaking a cell phone?
Chemical X: Yeah. What a sociopath.
TheGuardian: Who was he?
Chemical X: Do I get a reward or something?
TheGuardian: Fine. Give me your address and I'll bring it over.
Chemical X: Uh...never mind. His screen name was DrLethe. Creeped me out, dude. He was asking all kinds of questions about phreaking cell phones, particularly the Accelerama X27.

Same brand as the one Billy had used and the Surgeon had stolen.

Chemical X: I was bored, so I answered his questions, until he started majorly wigging on me. The questions were pretty basic. Wanted to know how the cells worked, if someone could trace them, etc. I'm not an accessory or anything, am I?
TheGuardian: Did you let him in the Network?
Chemical X: No! Like I said—sociopath. Kept

going on about how I'd be "smote" if I lied. Who the hell uses words like *smote* anymore?

When it became apparent that Chemical X didn't know any more about the mysterious DrLethe, Billy signed off, then fired up a password sniffer and a bot program that had been an early prototype of Interceptor.

It took him less than fifteen minutes to find two e-mail addresses, one for an individual who'd used DrLethe as a Network screen name, and another who'd gone by DrLethhe. He put the password sniffer to work on both, then sat back and waited.

BOROWSKI AND BRENTWOOD set out down the main path of the park, motioning to a handful of officers to fan out on the paths around them. Elizabeth Borkowski couldn't help but feel that they were looking for the needle in the proverbial haystack—just because this park fell in the center of the red circle on Billy's screen didn't mean this little jaunt in the park was the best use of taxpayer dollars. But Billy had been certain his program was about to zero in on this patch of green space, and—having heard her husband's stories of what his computer could do in college—she knew better than to dismiss him completely.

"This park's about a mile long, right?" James asked.

"One and four-tenths miles," she responded. The

park was quiet, except for the leaves rustling in the afternoon breeze and the sound of their shoes crunching on the wood chips lining the path.

She caught a glimpse of blue uniform over where she'd sent Ramirez and Cardenas. Turning her head, Elizabeth peered through the oak and cypress trees, but her colleague had disappeared down one of the other paths that snaked through the park.

"What is it?" Brentwood stopped and squinted in the direction in which she'd been looking.

"Eh, I think it was Ramirez." Elizabeth hadn't even realized she'd stopped walking. Man, this guy had her spooked. In her fifteen years of working with the MPD, she'd seen some brutal murders, but they'd all been committed in the heat of the moment or to achieve a specific end, like insurance money. This was the first time she'd encountered someone who took such obvious pleasure in killing women. Randomly.

They continued walking down the path, scanning between the trees and around the mossy trunks of fallen oaks decaying on the ground. Dry orange and brown leaves swirled around their legs.

A figure in black dropped out of the trees ahead of them.

Brentwood called out a warning. Elizabeth immediately went on full alert, her hands reaching for her gun as she planted her feet wide. But the man ahead of them had the draw on her. Time slowed to a crawl, and she was aware of everything around her—the sudden flight of crows from the twisted branches of the oak above them, the swirl of crackling leaves at her feet, James throwing his weight to the right as he prepared to dive in front of her, her gun hand rising slowly in front of her.

Elizabeth heard a soft ''ping'' come from the figure in front of her, his face obscured by black neoprene. He must've been using a silencer, she thought. And then she felt a sharp pain as something slammed into her shoulder.

The gun fell from her hand. Her body spun around from the bullet's force, and her arms windmilled in the air to break her fall. She hit the dirt hard, taking the brunt of the fall on her burning shoulder and the heel of one hand. Her hair fell into her eyes. She heard the gun fire again.

Pushing off on her bleeding hands, she faltered as her injured shoulder caused her arm to buckle. She tried again, this time resting her weight solely on her good arm. Lifting her torso, Elizabeth looked to the side just in time to see James fall beside her. His head rolled to the side. His eyes were wide open and glazed. He'd lost his glasses.

And then she was yelling at the top of her lungs, screaming for her partner, screaming at the man with the gun. Gun. She tried to get up, but her body was too weak from losing blood, staining the wood chips beneath her a dark red. She scrabbled in the dirt, trying desperately to turn her body around so she could find her weapon. God, not like this. She'd never wanted to go down like this. She couldn't lose her partner like this.

She reached out. Her hand closed over James's glasses.

A shadow fell over her. With one last burst of energy, she rolled to the side, the glasses clutched in her fist. The move took most of her energy, and it was all she could do to lie on her back and breathe. She looked up into the business end of a gun, held by a man she knew was the one they'd been searching for.

"Hello, Elizabeth," he said.

MAGGIE STARED at the photo, puzzling over the figures behind Billy. He hadn't known who they were or when the photo was taken, and if he didn't know, maybe she was grasping at straws. But she couldn't help but wonder if there wasn't something they were all missing.

"Hey, Maggie," Adriana chirped as she let herself in. She walked into the kitchen carrying a bag of fresh fruit from the local farmers' market. As soon as she'd deposited the bag on one of the counters, she came back into the living room and sat next to Maggie. Her hair had dark streaks of orange in it, which matched the quilt patches placed artfully on her vintage jeans. "What're you looking at?" she asked, leaning closer to see the photo.

"Just some pictures," Maggie mumbled absently. "Thanks for the fruit."

"Those peaches are to die for. Really." Her bracelets clicked against each other as she reached out to pull the photo closer to her. "Hey, who cut off James's head?"

Maggie nearly fell off the sofa. "What?"

Sitting back against the overstuffed cushions, Addy looked at her without a care in the world. "James. My boyfriend of several months. See that purple tie?" She tapped the surface of the photo with one red fingernail. "I bought him that for his birthday. Thought he needed a little color in his life."

Maggie glanced down at the hibiscuses and hula girls covering the retro design on Addy's three-quarter-length-sleeved shirt, a design that was topped off by a handful of artfully placed sequins. "I guess." She slid the picture back across the table so it was in front of her again. "Any idea who this is?" she asked.

Addy just smiled at her. "Elizabeth, of course. I bought her that purple shirt. Everything else the woman owns is in the gray family. Please. Boooring."

What if Billy really wasn't the target at all? What if the Surgeon really was sticking to his standard victim profile?

What if Detective Borkowski was his next target?

She shot off the couch, shouting for Billy.

"PING."

Billy pivoted in his seat and leaned forward to fix his gaze on the computer monitor. "Yes," he murmured under his breath. That polite "ping" meant the password sniffer had discovered the e-mail account and password for both DrLethe and DrLetthe. His fingers flew over the keyboard, and in seconds, Billy managed to log on to both accounts. DrLetthe was the virtual alter ego of a teenage X-Men fanatic who lived with his parents in Tuscaloosa. DrLethe, on the other hand, belonged to a 42-year-old man from Metairie, Louisiana, a suburb of New Orleans.

Elijah Carter. He finally had a name.

Billy had set a souped-up version of the Interceptor program—one that the FBI hadn't ever seen—in motion, hoping to dig up as much information on Carter as he could.

Then he heard Maggie call out to him, and the phone beside him rang shrilly.

MAGGIE SET THE PHONE in the hall back into its cradle. "He's got Elizabeth," she said, feeling dazed, empty. She watched, helpless, as all the color drained from Billy's face, and she felt a terrible, gut-wrenching guilt at all she'd brought into those people's lives. People who'd only tried to help her.

"Brentwood?" Billy asked. He sounded as though he was choking on the question.

Maggie could only shake her head. How would she ever tell Adriana? Her friend stood at her side, biting her glossy bottom lip, waiting to lend what comfort she could, if Maggie needed it. She didn't realize she was the one who would need comforting.

"Addy." Her voice cracked on the name. She wished to heaven she could just freeze this moment, where her friend was in love and happy and secure in her mostly wonderful life. But she couldn't, and she knew it would be unfair to prolong the news.

''What?'' Adriana said. But then Maggie turned and looked her straight in the eye, and somehow, Addy knew. She pressed a hand to her chest, shaking her head.

There was a knock at the door. Coward that she was, Maggie reached for the handle and opened it. The Monterey police detective named Daniel Cardenas stepped inside, his skin pale as though from some kind of shock.

Maggie knew what kind of shock.

''I'm looking for Ms. Torres,'' he said.

A low moan escaped from Adriana. ''Daniel.'' She shook her head, holding a hand out in front of her as if trying to ward off the horrible news she knew was coming.

''Adriana, we lost him,'' Detective Cardenas said. The corners of his mouth pulled back, and his eyes grew bright. ''I can't tell you—'' He broke off, unable to continue.

''Oh, James,'' Adriana said. She flattened her palms against her cheeks, her chest heaving with each breath. ''Oh, no.''

Maggie reached for her, catching Addy when her knees buckled. With Detective Cardenas's assistance, she gently deposited Addy in a chair and knelt next to her on the floor.

And then whatever shred of disbelief Addy had been clinging to dissolved, and she cried in great, heart-breaking sobs, her arms reaching out for the man she loved and grasping only air.

AS MUCH AS IT TORE her heart out to leave Addy alone during the worst time of her life, Maggie sent her friend away with Detective Cardenas. Both he and Billy agreed that any woman in contact with Maggie was in serious danger, and they knew they needed to get Addy as far away from Monterey as possible. So Cardenas wrapped her in his jacket and practically carried her to his car, assuring Maggie that he would put her on a plane to her parents' house in Baton Rouge, Louisiana, that evening.

And then Maggie's thoughts turned to Borkowski. It had been two hours since the no-nonsense detective had disappeared, and unfortunately, Maggie knew exactly what was probably happening to her right now. If she were still alive.

She gritted her teeth, putting the thought out of her mind. They had a window of only a few hours in which to find her. Dwelling on the details wasn't going to achieve that.

The sound of someone clearing his throat diverted her attention. She turned to find Billy holding the receiver of her hallway phone. Without thinking, she reached out to take it.

"Call my cell phone," he said. "Maybe he'll answer."

A long shot? Wishful thinking? Maybe, but right now it was all they had.

"His name is Elijah Carter," Billy said.

Or, maybe not.

"How did you—?"

"Call him." Billy spun around and stalked away, a dark look on his face. "I'll listen from the kitchen phone," he called over his shoulder.

Maggie looked down at the receiver. Call him. As if it were that easy. Call and talk again to the man who had tortured her, who had killed Billy's sister and ten other women, who had shot James Brentwood dead and who now had his partner at his mercy.

Maggie punched in the numbers.

To her shock, someone answered. "Well, Maggie. I was hoping you'd call."

She shuddered, feeling suddenly that there wasn't enough air in the room to breathe. "Let Elizabeth go," she said. "She has a family. Two little boys who need their mother."

"Nice," he drawled. He wasn't using the voice disguiser this time, and she found his high-pitched, breathless words even creepier than when he had used one. "Personalize the victim. Make her seem human to the big, bad killer instead of a nameless, faceless source of rage. I like it."

The room was starting to spin. She closed her eyes. "Let her go. Take me instead."

"Why, Maggie, how noble."

"Listen to me. *Let. Her. Go.* You know you want me instead," she snapped. Stop spinning, please, stop the world from spinning.

"Temper, temper," he said. "Maybe I'll come get you and we can have a party."

"You couldn't handle me and you know it, otherwise you'd be here by now."

He didn't respond. This was good. If she taunted him enough, maybe he'd come after her. Maybe it would buy them time.

She heard Elizabeth scream.

"Don't worry. Elizabeth and I haven't even gotten started yet. I might keep her around for a while."

"You needed drugs to get me last time, and you needed a gun to take down Elizabeth and James. You're just a sad, pathetic little man who needs a knife to make him feel powerful. And you'll never, ever take me," she snarled. "Not with guns, not with knives and definitely not with your bare hands."

Silence.

"There's a message for you on my front door, if you're man enough to come get it." She paused. "Elijah Carter." She hung up, the bells of the phone jangling from the impact.

Billy was already right beside her, obviously having come through in the middle of the conversation. "What are you doing?"

Without answering him, she grabbed a framed photo of herself and one of her aunt's off the telephone table. She yanked the back off the frame and pulled out the photo, tearing it neatly in half so her aunt was on one piece, and she was on the other. A brutal echo of the picture Billy carried in his wallet.

"What the hell do you think you're doing?" Billy asked again. He followed her into the kitchen, where her hand closed over one of the knives in the butcher block next to the stove. She pulled out the biggest and sharpest, then marched to the front of the house. Yanking open the front door, she chunked the knife through the picture of herself, impaling it to the wood.

Billy's hand closed around her wrist. "No, you are not going to do this," he snarled.

"You don't get it, do you?" she said, desperation welling up inside her, threatening to spill out of her in waves. "He's not going to stop. He will never stop until it's just him and me, alone."

She shook off his hand and took two large strides until she was standing at the end of the porch, her vision blurred by sudden tears. Out of the corner of her eye, she saw him motion to the two cops watching the house to move to the back door. They quickly complied.

"He'll kill my friends," she continued. "He'll kill my family, he'll kill everyone and anyone I've ever loved." She whirled around to face him. "I've ruined Adriana's life. Elizabeth is in horrible pain right now because of me." She stepped backward onto the first step. She didn't care. "He'll kill her, he'll come after Addy, and he'll kill you if you stand in his way." Her chest was heaving, and her breath caught in sobs. She was behaving insanely. She didn't care.

"Mags." Billy moved toward her, one hand reaching out for her. She lurched back, onto the second step. She didn't deserve that kind of concern. She didn't deserve to have him touch her.

"Get out of here, Billy. Just go. Revenge isn't worth your life. Look at what he's done to Addy, to

James, to Gina and Abigail.'' She dropped onto the third step. ''Don't stay here. I'm not worth your life.''

''I'm not going anywhere,'' he said.

''If Jenna is all that matters, then Jenna would want you to live. She'd want you away from here.'' With that, Maggie stumbled forward, not knowing where she was headed or why. A few steps later, and she was standing in the middle of her front yard, the street and the trees on the other side in plain view.

Billy was still there, just a step behind her, waiting to catch her when she cracked.

''Oh,'' she said, looking around. ''I'm outside.'' The world tilted slightly on its axis and righted itself again.

''Yeah, you are,'' he replied.

''I need to go back.'' She felt so small, standing here under the overcast afternoon sky.

''Then come here, Mags,'' he said.

She took a halting step toward him. For the first time in a year and a half, she could see her neighbor's house.

Billy backed away.

''Oh, no, Billy…'' Her hands reached for him, but he shifted, eluding her grasp.

''Come on. You can walk back.''

Clenching her teeth, she took another step, and damn him, he moved again. She heard the screech of a seagull overhead, and her entire body jolted in surprise.

''Look at me, Mags,'' he said. Returning her gaze to him, she saw that he was tapping the bone underneath one of his unfathomable gray eyes. "Just look at me."

"I hate this," she ground out. She moved her right foot a few inches forward.

"I know. Just a couple more steps."

Inch by agonizing inch, Maggie made her way across the yard, her eyes never leaving Billy's. And then, suddenly, she was at the porch again, and he was holding her in his arms. Well, if that little show didn't convince him she was a raving lunatic, she didn't know what would, she thought.

With a gentleness that brought tears to her eyes, he took her hand and led her up the stairs. "Come inside, Maggie," he said. "You're going to be okay."

Chapter Thirteen

"Are you out of your mind, or do you just enjoy thumbing your nose at authority, Agent Corrigan?" Special Agent in Charge Fay Parker loomed in the doorway of Maggie's house, the padded shoulders of her dark-gray power suit making her look even more formidable. She stepped inside and, with a surprising about-face, approached Maggie. "You must be the infamous Maggie Reyes," she said, extending her hand.

"That's me, although I'm not so sure of the infamous part." Maggie shook Parker's hand, surprised when the woman opted for a gentle yet firm grip instead of a bone-crushing hold. She looked like the bone-crushing type.

Parker's iron-gray bob swung along her jawline as she whirled on Billy, the warmth that had been in her eyes turning to exasperation. "You couldn't leave it alone, could you, John Wayne?" she said.

"No, ma'am," he replied, unflinching. Maggie would have flinched. Big time. Agent Parker, with her booming smoker's voice and that icy schoolteacher stare, could frighten anyone into submission with just a look. But Billy seemed unfazed.

In his hand was a sheaf of papers on which he'd printed the information on Elijah Carter that his computer had spat out. Parker gestured toward it. "So I hear our guy has a name. Tell me what you know about Mr. Carter."

Not even bothering to ask how Parker had gleaned that information so quickly, Billy began reading from the top of the stack. "Elijah Carter was born in Metairie, Louisiana, to a Southern Baptist minister and his wife. By all accounts, he had a healthy childhood until his father died when he was four. Shortly thereafter, his mother remarried and, together with her husband, co-founded the Church of the Collective."

"The Collective?" Maggie interrupted. "But that's that religious cult—the one that made the followers wear ashes on their faces and forbade all activities except for reading, sleeping and praying to whatever god it was they worshipped."

Billy nodded. "And Carter's stepfather, Morris Carter, was as strict as they come. His neighbors called the police a couple of times because they heard him beating Elijah and his wife, but no one ever pressed charges."

"And so little Elijah grew up hating women," Parker said. "Because his mother's marriage to a monster was the ultimate betrayal."

"The Collective was particularly strict with the rules it imposed on women," Maggie said, wrapping her arms around herself. "They were almost vilified for being a source of sin and temptation. Seems some of Morris's teaching stuck with his stepson after all.''

Billy nodded, then continued. "Elijah was something of a genius, if a little sullen in school. After graduation, he enlisted in the army, specializing in computer surveillance.'' Billy glanced up at Parker. ''Old-school techniques from the late 80s. He was dishonorably discharged in May of 1990 after one of his fellow enlisted colleagues accused him of backhanding her when they were out on a date. Most of his coworkers said he was quiet and kept to himself, though he sometimes seemed 'a little odd.''' He shuffled the papers around and then continued. ''After that, he just took the odd low-level computer tech job here and there.''

''Well,'' Parker grunted. ''As much as it pains me to give you even faint praise for bending the rules, it seems your work here has mended some fences with the Monterey Chief of Police after that snafu we had last August. Your Detective Borkowski called the Violent Crimes Division and asked for backup.'' She sighed, setting her heavy briefcase down with a thud. ''Which means I can't kick your ass six ways to Sunday like I'd planned, but I am here to check up on you.''

Billy raised an eyebrow, and Maggie stepped closer to him, putting a hand on his elbow.

''I'm going to stick to you like a burr on a donkey's butt, Agent Corrigan,'' Parker continued, her statement matter-of-fact, but still delivered like a whip-crack. ''You may be in this up to your neck, but you're not going to go all renegade and throw your life away. I'm bringing you back home, son, if I have to die trying."

The corners of Billy's mouth tightened, and his brow furrowed slightly. Although the relationship between him and Parker looked professional and even adversarial on the surface, it was clear that there was something deeper, almost familial, at its core. "That won't be necessary, ma'am."

Her speech finished, Parker relaxed the rigid set of her shoulders and flicked her gaze to Maggie's hand, resting lightly on Billy's elbow. "No," she said carefully. "Maybe not."

With that, she snapped her head up to Maggie's face. "Well, Ms. Reyes. Since we're here to provide assistance, why don't you brief me as to why there's an ugly-looking knife stuck in your door?"

ONCE AGENT PARKER and Monterey PD Detective Daniel Cardenas heard about Maggie's plan to use herself as bait, her fate was sealed. It took some convincing, but eventually the detective newly put in charge of the case and the veteran FBI agent realized that using Maggie as bait was one of their only options, if they wanted to close the case quickly. In a matter of hours, a small group of FBI agents and plainclothes Monterey police officers had arrived and were taking up their posts around the area. Unfortunately, the area directly in front of Maggie's house offered little cover for law enforcement to hide in, so they scattered among the trees across the street and in the yards of her closest neighbors. Which still felt too far away.

In the few hours they had left before nightfall, Cardenas and Billy telephoned hotels and rental agencies, asking if anyone had come across someone named Elijah Carter.

At 3:57 p.m., they got a yes.

Cardenas and a few of his people went to the Celebrity Motel, a mere five blocks from Iris Canyon Park. They burst into Room 226, guns drawn, only to find a small suitcase and a piece of blue material on the brown and orange bedspread.

At 4:16 p.m., someone called Maggie's phone and hung up.

At 7:12 p.m., a call came in that a female stabbing victim had been found lying near the side of Highway 1.

Maggie dropped the phone as soon as the detective on the other end had hung up. "They found Borkowski," she said.

All of the blood left Billy's angular face. "Is she—?"

"She's alive," Maggie broke in quickly, "but barely. Cardenas said the police are combing the scene, and she's on her way to the hospital."

Billy looked away, his jaw working furiously.

"Billy, she had a heart-shaped locket around her neck."

"Jenna's?" he asked.

"I don't know," she replied. "But there was a note. Detective Cardenas wouldn't tell me what it said over the phone, but I got a feeling it was a goodbye letter.'' She closed her eyes, feeling sick over what she was about to say. ''They said your sister signed it.''

Myriad emotions crossed Billy's face, each more heart-breaking than the last.

Maggie's instincts were screaming at her, telling her this was one of Carter's misdirections, but she couldn't stand the pain on Billy's face. He so clearly wanted to leave. And, after all, it was probably better that he did.

She touched his arm. ''Cardenas says you're welcome at the scene.''

He closed his eyes, his hands clenching and unclenching. What she wouldn't have done to take some of that pain away from him.

''I'm not leaving you alone,'' he finally said. But he wouldn't look at her.

She stepped closer to him, her body nearly touching his. ''I'm not. There are police and FBI everywhere,'' she said, although she knew that many of them would have been diverted to the crime scene where they'd found Borkowski. ''Go. I'll be fine.'' *Stay,* she wanted to say instead. *Choose me.* But Jenna was what mattered. He'd been wrong, on that night not so long ago—Maggie couldn't save him, not when she couldn't even come close to saving herself. Maybe something in Jenna's note would give him the peace he so desperately needed. And when this was all over, if she were still standing, they could sort out the rest.

His gray eyes opened, and the hopelessness in them made her long to throw her arms around him. But she wasn't about to hold him here. "Go," she said again.

The ache in her chest grew stronger when Billy turned and walked out of her house. Was she keeping him out of danger, or putting him in it? She wasn't sure. But she knew that after her challenge to Elijah Carter on the telephone, he'd want to come after her tonight. And he might be more likely to do so if he saw her in the house alone.

Of course, there were three police guards patrolling the perimeter around her house and dozens of others further out, in the trees, down the street. Fortunately, every single one of them was doing their best to stay invisible. To all outside observers, she was alone.

And scared beyond belief. She went to the locked secretary near the fireplace in her living room and unlocked the top drawer. Pulling out the Glock, she checked the safety and loaded it up with a fresh clip, then strapped the holster around her body and stuffed the gun inside. And then, once again, Maggie waited.

TWO HOURS LATER Maggie was in the kitchen when one of the police officers walked past her window. The security lights illuminated his black uniform, though he kept his face turned away from her.

Dropping the book she'd been pretending to read on the table, Maggie stared at him as he ambled across the sand and groundcover plants. Something was wrong. He wasn't trying to conceal himself.

Billy hadn't yet returned, and the MPD personnel

and FBI agents who surrounded her home weren't keeping in contact with her—Cardenas had seen no reason to allow her access to their radio transmissions. And here she was, face-to-face with either the stupidest police officer on the planet, or the most dangerous man in the city.

The man slipped back into shadow, and for ten interminable minutes, all was quiet outside and in. She listened for breaking glass, snapping locks, squeaking hinges, but she heard nothing.

Fifteen minutes later, the situation hadn't changed.

She wondered if she should signal the MPD—if she felt she was in trouble, she was supposed to let them know through the wire she was wearing. But Maggie knew they wouldn't get a second chance if she called them in too early, so she waited.

Still nothing.

"Now I know how he gets his victims—he bores them to death," she said, just to dispel the oppressive silence that was hanging like fog inside her house. She focused on the area just outside her window, her fingers touching the light switch. While the circle of brilliant light from the security lamps extended about three feet outside her house, she couldn't see the ocean beyond them. So she just listened to the muffled roar of the waves. And she waited.

A knock sounded at her front door.

She turned into the hallway, but before she could reach the doorway, the knob turned, and a SWAT officer stepped into her home. She could have sworn she'd locked that door.

The man grinned at her, his face partially obscured by black camouflage paint, and his eyes unnaturally bright. She knew those eyes.

"Thanks for inviting me in," he said. Her photo fell out of his gloved hand and fluttered to the ground. He held the knife in his hand.

"Maggie Reyes, requesting assistance," she said aloud.

"They're not coming. I took care of that." He stepped toward her. "All of the Adversary's little friends hiding in the trees. Gone, gone, gone."

Backing into the kitchen, Maggie stretched one arm behind her, to get at the Glock that was tucked into the inner pants holster in the small of her back.

She drew the gun. With lightening quickness, he threw a knife. It whirled through the air and hit her square in the shoulder, only nicking her skin, but the blow zinged through the nerve endings of her arm, and she dropped the Glock on the tiles.

Stupid, stupid woman.

"The Adversary is slow. She will be taken easily," he said, the statements all the more chilling for their bizarreness. "A good soldier knows how to take down even the most worthy enemy."

She stumbled away from him, holding her injured arm in an instinctive attempt to immobilize her shoulder. The sound of metal singing against leather made her turn around, and she saw that the Surgeon had a new knife in his possession—a wicked-looking hunting knife with a serrated edge on top. She knew that knife.

"The red days are here, and the Adversary must be cleansed of her sins."

She backed against the kitchen table, the wood hitting against her spine. Blood dripped down her arm, seeping through the thick material of her sweater.

Nowhere to run.

Any minute now, he'd come at her, hoping to take her down with one blow. She stared at him, fear holding her limbs paralyzed. He was here. She was alone.

"The Adversary must go under the knife," he said, his breath whistling through his nose.

He stepped toward her, the knife glinting under the lights of her kitchen. He'd taken her by surprise in New Orleans. This time, he was walking directly toward her, and still she didn't have a prayer. He was in her house. The police weren't coming. No one was coming. And she...couldn't...move.

"Pain," he breathed, still smiling obscenely at her through the black makeup. "Pain will set all enemies free. It will—"

Suddenly, the glass patio doors shattered into a million pieces, the violent sound of breaking glass obscuring the Surgeon's next words. Taking advantage of the distraction, Maggie pulled one of the kitchen chairs in an arc around her body and shoved it at Carter.

As tiny, brilliant shards rained down on the kitchen floor, the figure that had crashed through the patio doors rolled on the tiles to a standing position, and then, with lightning speed, dove for the man in black.

Billy.

He landed a hard punch on the side of the killer's jaw, and then, with one hand clamped around the Surgeon's knife arm, he delivered a series of jabs to the man's stomach. The killer doubled over, but then he pulled his knife-hand free, slashing at Billy's torso with wide, controlled movements. Billy backed away.

Oh, God, he was going to get himself killed. She shoved another chair at the Surgeon, hoping to throw the man off balance. He kicked the chair away. She scanned the floor for her gun.

Just as she found it, she saw a black-gloved hand reach down and grab it. Inside of a heartbeat, he straightened, pointed, aimed. With a crack, the gun fired, and Billy spun around from the impact.

Oh, no.

The bullet crashed into the upper part of his chest. The Surgeon fired again, just as Billy's body smacked against the floor. In a matter of seconds, the side of his face was covered in blood.

Billy. Her vision narrowed, and the world started to spin around her as mind and body threatened to shut down completely. *No no no no no.* She shook her head violently and stumbled forward to where Billy lay as still as death on the tile floor. She willed him to get up, not able to believe that he might be…could be…

His chest rose as he took a breath.

Alive.

She had to get out of here, get the Surgeon away from him.

With all the strength she had left, Maggie turned

to face the man who had shot Billy. "Elijah Carter!" she called. Behind her, she could hear the sound of the ocean, coming at her full volume from beyond her shattered patio doors. A chill wind blew through the opening, lifting her hair and caressing the back of her neck.

The Surgeon whirled around.

"Why don't you run?" she asked.

And then, with a prayer on her lips, she tore across the room and through the gaping hole, her shoes crunching down on shards of broken glass. The clouds that had been covering the moon shifted, and the sand was bathed in a blue-gray light. She followed the moon across the sand, down the beach.

Billy. She had to keep him away from Billy.

She shouted for help from any of the MPD officers who might still be nearby. The sand sucked at her feet as if to pull her under, but she ran until her muscles burned, the wind tearing at her hair and clothes. Behind her, she could hear the killer who had pursued and terrified her for eighteen months following her over the sound of the crashing waves. She headed for the rocks.

The sand slowed her down, sticking to her shoes and giving way beneath her feet like thick mud. She could hear him getting closer, and she knew she'd have to make a choice soon. Keep running until he caught her, or turn and face him on her terms.

You only run from what you can't see.

Reaching the jagged black rocks, she clambered up the side of one, scrabbling for hand and foot holds as her breath came out in ragged gasps. When she reached the top, she glanced down to the roiling inlet of water that surrounded her rock and several others like it. The water surged and foamed inside the small cove, the motion making it appear pitch-black in color.

On the other side of her, a wave crashed against the rock, spraying her with a fine mist. In the dim light, she saw the Surgeon climbing up the rock to face her.

As he pulled himself to the top, she reached down, and her hand closed over a loose stone covered with a hundred jagged edges. She threw it at him, catching him square in the face.

With a roar, he rose to his feet, blood running between the fingers of the hand that clutched his face.

He was a man. Not the Surgeon, but Elijah Carter. She could see him clearly in the moonlight, and he was just a man who could bleed. She had made him bleed. The black cap had fallen off his head, revealing a scrub of light hair in a military precision cut. He was shorter than she'd expected.

The wind tugged several strands of her hair loose from her ponytail, and tendrils whipped across her face. She stood on the rock, with the whole wide open outdoors around her, and the fear didn't consume her. She was alive, for this moment, and she wasn't about to go down without a fight. She might get hurt, she might die, but she wouldn't ever, ever let this Elijah Carter have a hold on her nightmares again.

"I'm not afraid of you, Carter," she yelled over the surf. "You stupid, pathetic little man. I'll never be afraid of you."

He shouted at her in incoherent rage. He was still holding his face, and he was limping slightly—Billy had managed to hurt him, too.

She braced herself for impact, hoping that with her martial arts training, she'd be lucky enough to survive this. To get back to Billy.

Billy.

The thought of him lying in her kitchen, unconscious and bleeding, twisted her heart. She had to live through this. She had to get back to him.

Out of the corner of her eye, she noticed something crawling over the edge of the rock. Before she could register what was happening, Billy lunged at the Surgeon, landing a heavy punch on the man's injured cheek. He hit him again, and Carter reeled back from the blow. Carter swung at him, but Billy feinted and whirled around with dizzying speed, delivering a roundhouse kick to the man's solar plexus.

Carter stood at the edge of the rock, his arms windmilling in the air. With one last punch, Billy sent him reeling back. Carter's body arced through the air with a slow gracefulness, then he slipped into the water. It surged around him, and within seconds, the undertow had pulled him to the depths below. And then Elijah Carter, aka the Surgeon, disappeared beneath the waves without a trace.

Maggie ran to Billy and threw her arms around him.

"Oh, Billy. You're alive," she said, her breath ragged with emotion.

He held her to him, stroking her hair. "I thought I'd lost you," he said.

She ran her hands along his back and shoulders, as if reassuring herself that he really was here, and whole. Her hands found the telltale bumps of a Kevlar vest underneath his clothes. Thank God. Then she leaned away from him to inspect his head wound, grateful again to find it was only a scratch.

"What about the police?" she asked, dreading the answer. "Where are they?"

"I found a couple when I approached the house. They were fine—just knocked unconscious. I'm betting he used stealth to slip past the rest."

She blew out a relieved breath and wrapped her arms around him again, afraid that the strength of the emotion she felt would overwhelm her.

"I can't believe you came back," she said.

"I never left," he said into her hair.

She pulled back, looking directly into his gray eyes as the wind whistled around them, tugging out the rubber band that held her hair back. Black curls whipped into her eyes, and she reached up to shove them away. "Never left...." she repeated, sounding rather stupid to her own ears. But his statement left her dumbfounded.

Another wave hit the rock, sending up a spray of water. He turned his body to shield her from it. "I had the same thought you did, that the Surgeon would be more likely to show if he thought you were alone in the house. And I thought the locket and note might have been an attempt to mislead us. So, at your request, I left you alone. And then I watched you from the rocks outside.''

''What about...?'' She stopped, unable to speak.

''Jenna?'' he asked gently. ''She's gone. And tonight, you were all that mattered.'' He paused, and then, ''I'm in love with you, Mags.'' He stepped closer, into her space, taking one of her hands and placing it on his chest. ''You're in my heart,'' he said, echoing the words he'd spoken to her a few nights before.

''You took away the nightmares,'' she whispered.

He pulled her closer. ''And your hair is still the most erotic thing I've ever seen,'' he whispered, plunging his hands into it before lowering his mouth to hers.

The sounds of the FBI and police officers running toward them made them come up for air. Billy jumped off the rock and then helped her climb down. ''Hey, are you all right?'' he asked, concern for her written all over his face. ''Should I get you back inside?''

She leaned her head back, taking in the night sky for the fist time in eighteen months without a sheet of glass between it and herself. She thought about the answer for a moment, as the waves surged around her and the fall breeze pulled and tugged at her hair and clothes.

''No,'' she finally said. ''I'm fine here.'' And she wrapped her arms around his waist and pulled him close.

Epilogue

Seven months later.

As Billy had predicted, Elijah Carter had slipped past most of the Monterey Police Department to reach Maggie. Two officers died that night, and the two that Billy had found sustained severe concussions that eventually healed. Carter himself was declared dead after a search party failed to recover his body from the black water.

Although consumed by grief at losing James Brentwood, Adriana Torres returned to California and threw herself into her work, her normally effervescent personality subdued, but still visible if you looked hard enough. Per Honduran custom, she replaced the bright colors and loud prints of her wardrobe with somber grays and blacks, which Maggie told Billy she would wear for at least a year. Maggie checked up on her every day, bringing her outside into the sunlight as often as possible. Sometimes, Billy himself would visit Adriana, and the two of them would talk about James.

Elizabeth Borkowski's wounds healed, and though the Chief of Police made her see the police psychologist, she was back to her wisecracking self in no time. She gave a moving eulogy at James Brentwood's funeral, and soon she was back working cases for the MPD. No one but Billy, Maggie and her husband knew that she sometimes burst into tears when she thought she was alone, missing her partner of twelve years.

Billy reached into his pocket and pulled out the locket he'd been carrying with him since Detective Cardenas had returned it to him. The note from Jenna had been a fake, planted, as he'd suspected, in an attempt to misdirect the police. But the locket was real. He snapped the catch and the gold heart split open, revealing a tiny photo in each side—his mother and his father. He pulled the chain straight between his fingers and looped it around a gold picture frame that held an image of his sister, allowing the open locket to dangle from one corner. Maggie had found some negatives in some boxes inside one of his closets, and she'd replaced the family photos he'd destroyed years ago. He was glad.

Inhaling deeply, he stepped back to look at the images of his family. It still hurt, but the pain was bearable now, softened by time and healing.

He felt a pair of arms skim his sides to wrap around his waist, and then a small body pressed against his back, covering him in warmth. He covered one of Maggie's hands with his own, his fingers brushing against the diamond ring he'd placed there just a few days before.

She was healing; so was he.

"You okay?" she asked, leaning around him to look him in the eye without letting him go.

He smiled down at her, happy for the first time in years.

"I know," she said, her brown eyes sparkling. "I love you, too."

She stepped around him, her hair frothing in dark curls around her fine-boned face, traces of pink sunburn on her nose and cheeks. "Come on," she said, holding out her hand. "Let's go outside."

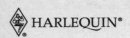

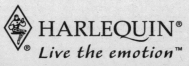

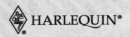

HARLEQUIN®

INTRIGUE®

**presents a new force of rugged lawmen
who abide by their own rules...**

COWBOY COPS

They live—they love—by the code of the West.

A riveting new promotion featuring
men branded by the badge!

BEHIND THE SHIELD by Sheryl Lynn
March 2004

RESTLESS SPIRIT by Cassie Miles
April 2004

OFFICIAL DUTY by Doreen Roberts
May 2004

DENIM DETECTIVE by Adrienne Lee
June 2004

Available at your favorite retail outlet.

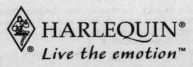

HARLEQUIN®
Live the emotion™

Visit us at www.eHarlequin.com

HICC2

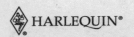

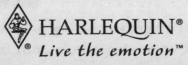